THE BEAST MEN

AIRSHIP 27 PRODUCTIONS

Quatermain: The New Adventures- The Beast Men
© 2018 Wayne Carey

Published by Airship 27 Productions
www.airship27.com
www.airship27hangar.com

Interior illustrations © 2018 Clayton Hinkle
Cover illustration © 2018 Graham Hill

Editor: Ron Fortier
Associate Editor: Fred Adams Jr.
Marketing and Promotions Manager: Michael Vance
Production and design by Rob Davis.

ISBN-13: 978-1-946183-33-0
ISBN-10: 1-946183-33-4

Printed in the United States of America

10 9 8 7 6 5 4 3 2 1

QUATERMAIN

THE NEW ADVENTURES

THE BEAST MEN
BY WAYNE CAREY

CHAPTER ONE

I have come into the habit in my old age of putting down into writing the various adventures in which I have played a small part throughout my life. As with many of the others, the one I am about to recount may be considered unbelievable, but I assure the reader that it did happen. Since there are some more sensitive expositions, my hope is that this does not become public until well after I and most principle players are long gone from this world.

My involvement began while on a hunting trip on the Highveld with an American by the name of Jacob Kennedy, whom I met shortly after returning to England to live in Yorkshire following the discovery of King Solomon's mines. Kennedy was a distant relative of my good friend Sir Henry Curtis, and it was at Sir Henry's estate that he learned of my previous vocation as a trader and hunter in Africa. His own occupation as a cattleman in Texas provided him the opportunity to see the great American West, where he delighted in hunts for elk, bear, bison, and cougar. His greatest desire was to travel to Africa where he might hunt elephant, buffalo, and lion. Sir Henry assured him that no other guide would do but me, though I sought retirement with my newly gained wealth. I had not yet settled into my new life as an English country gentleman and was restless for the home I had known most of my life, at least for one last time. There were matters to settle in Durban, Natal, one of them being the disposition of my old house, though in all honesty my solicitor there could have dealt with the issues. My son Harry was financially secure for his studies at medical college. Zululand was under the authority of the Crown as colonial territory, although there were rumors of squabbles between tribal leaders vying to replace the deposed Zulu king, Cetewayo, who was also in England at the time, though our paths did not cross until I returned to Africa a few years later, but that is another story. The conflict with the Boers had just settled, with the independence of Transvaal. The region seemed quiet, at least for the time being. To leave England for a few months would be a small matter. Therefore, as I found Mr. Kennedy a congenial companion, I decided to take him up on his request. Sir Henry initially planned on joining us, but later declined due to other commitments. So Kennedy and I began the long voyage to the Cape, then to my home in Natal, where we arranged our expedition, and finally into the interior for a hunt of trophies.

I enlisted the assistance of Mnqoba, whom I had known since he was a child at my father's mission. We had been on many hunts over the years, and he aided in hiring some of the local men for the trip. With two wagons drawn by oxen teams and horses for the American and myself, we set off.

Although Kennedy was an agreeable man, very well read and good in conversation, he often allowed his arrogance to get the better of him. He was not a braggart, as some gentlemen hunters are wont to be, but he believed that his experiences in the wild American West provided him with enough knowledge to forge ahead on his own. I became frustrated when I would explain how something is usually done, and he would do what his own mind was set upon. I decided that we would make an early end to the trip and find his trophies as soon as possible. Not that I did not enjoy his companionship, but in the actual hunt he became stubborn and thick headed. That allows for danger to enter.

A week into the trip, we followed a small herd of elephants along a rocky ridge. The spoor showed that the elephants, probably half a dozen, were some hours away, but we came across a herd of greater kudu feeding on shrubs among the clusters of baobab trees. The kudu were skittish, although we were downwind and our horses and wagons were some distance away. We were extremely quiet, there being Kennedy, myself, Mnqoba, and two other men, the rest remaining with the wagons. I have seen antelope anxious in this way when a predator was near, before it is scented or seen. Before I could utter a word of caution, Kennedy sighted a buck and took it down, sending the whole herd to flight across the grassland.

I sent one of the men on a run back to the wagons to bring them up, so that we might follow the elephant spore. Kennedy went on ahead to secure his kill.

The buck had fallen near a scraggly baobab tree about a hundred yards away. As he approached it, something large and dark slunk from behind the thick bough of the tree and pounced upon the dead kudu. Kennedy was within a few yards of it by that time and came up short, blocking my own view of the scene.

He fumbled with his rifle, but the black shape charged him, emitting a vicious, piercing scream unlike any growl I have ever heard. Kennedy went down under the impact, his rifle firing into the air.

I could finally see that it was a panther, but larger than any I have encountered.

Lifting my own rifle, I took aim on the creature's broad head as it tore into Kennedy. The shot was a difficult one due to the animal's movements and the fact that I had to act swiftly. I squeezed the trigger, and the bullet caught it in the shoulder. The results were satisfying, for the strike knocked it free of its victim.

As Mnqoba and I ran toward Kennedy, the creature stood upon its hind legs, growled hideously, and bounded through the brush and up the rocky slope.

Kennedy lay unconscious, his chest raked with claw marks, his throat torn with fangs. His tattered clothes turned red with his blood, yet he still breathed. I tended to him while Mnqoba called to our other man to hurry the wagons. There was a kraal a few miles to the south, and if we could get him there quickly, there might still be hope.

"What attacked him, Macumazahn?" Mnqoba asked. He pulled some cloth from a skin bag he carried over his shoulder, bent down, a pressed the bundled cloth against Kennedy's neck, stanching the flow of blood.

"A panther," I said.

"Nay, Macumazahn, that was no panther to stand up on hind legs. That was a devil."

Leaving Mnqoba to apply pressure to the wound, I picked up my rifle with bloodstained hands and checked the chamber. "Don't be ridiculous. That was a panther. I grant you it was larger than any I have seen, and deformed, but a panther nonetheless. Does a devil bleed, Mnqoba? Or leave tracks? Look." I pointed to claw marks upon the stones and paw prints in the dirt, as well as drops of bright red blood leading away from the wounded man and the dead kudu.

"It may be flesh and blood, but it is still a devil."

"That doesn't even make sense, Mnqoba."

"Or perhaps a *tokoloshe*."

"A what?"

"A *tokoloshe*. They are created by witch doctors who have been offended. They look like bears and aren't very big, but maybe this is close enough. Or an *imbulu*, but they tend to be like a lizard and can turn into a human, though the tail always remains."

"Stop talking nonsense, Mnqoba. That was a panther. It's wounded. I can't allow a wounded animal roaming around with a kraal only a few miles away. Load Kennedy in the wagon as soon as it gets here while I follow its spoor and see if I can't dispatch it."

"No, Macumazahn. You will need my help. If a panther, you will need my gun. If a devil, you will need my prayers to Unkulunkulu." He often used the Zulu word for the Supreme Creator, the Great-Great, when he referred to God, and he still held to some old superstitions, as evidenced by his incoherent mumbling about mythical monsters, even though he had long ago converted to Christianity under my father's teachings.

"Stay with Kennedy. He'll die if you don't."

I climbed the rocks, following the spoor through the sparse shrub. Blood smeared over leaves and branches, claws scraped across rocky surfaces, and pads pressed into the occasional patches of soil. If I had to identify the animal by prints alone, I would have failed. Although the marks in the dirt were similar to a big cat, there were deformities that were inconsistent with either leopard or lion. They were unlike any prints I had seen before, but they were impressions made in the dirt and therefore there was nothing supernatural about the creature. It was solid and real, and a danger to others unless dispatched. Once killed, we could determine its origins.

I circled a particularly dense area of dried scrub, though the spoor led through these brambles.

Creeping over the stones, careful that my boots made little noise, I held my Winchester ready, my eyes catching every movement within the branches. It stood motionless, surprising me. I had been watching for some black shape low within the shadows of the scrub. I had not expected something taller than myself. It stepped out of the brush as I neared it, glaring at me eye to eye. It swung a forelimb and knocked the barrel of my rifle aside as I squeezed the trigger. Startled by the blast, it gave voice to a screeching growl inches from my face and I feared its long fangs would rip into my flesh, but it turned instantly and bounded away.

I gave chase, but now it moved quicker than I could limp. It was gone. Standing on the rock ridge, I scanned the rolling hills of the veldt and saw nothing of the creature. No doubt I could eventually find prints on the hard packed earth and bent or broken shafts of grass, but that would take time that Kennedy did not have.

"Did you get it, Macumazahn?" Mnqoba asked as I returned to find them loading Kennedy into one of the wagons.

"No," I said. "It got away."

"You saw it?"

"Yes."

"Was it a cat or a devil?"

Both, I would have said, but I did not want to encourage him. Plus, I was in doubt of my own eyes. How could I explain what I saw, standing in front of me, its green slit eyes even with my own, its sleek black fur covering the face and head of a huge cat, standing erect as a man, using forelimbs as a human would arms? And when it ran away, it had done so on its hind legs, before dropping to all fours. It was no cat as I have known them, yet I could not believe that it was supernatural. I have read the Scriptures all my life and listened to the teachings of my father, but no devil or demon had been described as what I had faced. What was it, then?

CHAPTER TWO

We traveled to the kraal of Bhekizizwe, where I had occasionally traded in my old life. I would have hoped for someone who knew modern medicine, like a visiting missionary, but we had to settle for the *inyanga*, a witch doctor, who at least had a vast understanding of herbal remedies. Mnqoba was not hopeful. Neither was I as I urged the oxen to their top speed. Kennedy had lost a lot of blood. If he survived till we reached the kraal, it would be a miracle. Mnqoba rode in the wagon, attempting to keep the poor man steady and stanch the flow of blood as best he could, while I drove the team. Our other men followed behind with the other wagon and the horses and were soon lost to view. They would eventually catch up with us.

Men from the kraal came out to greet us, having seen our hasty trek over the veldt and the subsequent dust cloud in our wake. They would have stopped our wagon but I yelled out to them as we approached.

"We have a wounded man!" I declared in Zulu. "He is dying and needs help."

Two men turned and raced back to the kraal, outdistancing our exhausted oxen. A third leaped nimbly onto the wagon, looked in at Mnqoba and Kennedy, gave me a grave nod, and settled on the box beside me.

I slowed the team down only after passing through the kraal's gate. The snorting, wheezing oxen stumbled, staggered, and eventually came to a halt. People crowded around us, and the man who sat beside me sprang from his seat and began shouting orders.

Climbing into the back of the wagon, I checked on Kennedy's labored breathing. His skin was ashen and cold. Many hands helped lift him from the back and bore him into a hut that was decorated with many talismans. The *inyanga* was an old man who sprang to life as he looked over Kennedy while he was carried into the hut, then he called over a young boy, his apprentice, and gave rapid instructions. The boy hurried to a garden next to the hut and began selecting certain herbs. The *inyanga* disappeared into the hut, chasing out all others but his young apprentice.

The crowd slowly began to disperse, but I called over the man who had ridden back with us.

"I am grateful for your help and that of your people," I said.

Reaching into the wagon, I pulled out the carcass of an antelope Kennedy had shot earlier in the day, now gutted and wrapped in canvass. I offered it as a gift for the witch doctor and the people of the kraal for their assistance. The man nodded gravely and took hold of the carcass, carrying it off.

The *inyanga* came out presently and approached me. "I have done what can be done, Macumazahn. He is badly injured and has lost much blood and is not long for this world. It is now up to the spirits whether he shall live or die, but I am afraid he has very little time left. I will stay with him to fight back the darkness until the very end."

I thanked him, knowing that Kennedy had very little hope of surviving under his primitive ministrations but had absolutely none had we tried to find an English doctor. Considering the damage that had been done and the loss of blood, I doubted a modern hospital could have helped.

He returned to the dark interior of his hut.

Word came to us that Chief Bhekizizwe wished to see us. Mnqoba and I were escorted to the largest of the huts at the far end of the kraal. Outside, the large, muscular man at least my own age, with white liberally sprinkling his dark curls, sat upon a stool, flanked by two of his warriors. Bhekizizwe had always treated me kindly and his village often traded with me or some of the other traders.

"*Sawubona*, Bhekizizwe," I said.

"*Sawubona*, Macumazahn," he replied. "My sorrow over your injured companion. Will he survive?"

"It does not look hopeful," I said.

"What happened?"

"He was attacked by a large panther. I was able to wound it and gave chase, but it escaped from us. We could not take the time to hunt it down because we needed to bring Mister Kennedy to help."

Bhekizizwe furrowed his brow. "Did you see this panther, Macumazahn?"

I shifted uncomfortably, not willing to describe the creature. "Yes."

"Where was this?"

I described the area to him.

"Odd," he said. "There has not been a panther near here since I was a child. Even leopards are rare. They will roam if game is scarce, but it is plentiful and they have kept to their territories north of us. But still no panther has been seen."

"I'll return in the morning and hunt it down," I said. "I don't want any wounded cat in your territory. It will be dangerous to anyone else."

"That will be good. Stay here tonight. I offer my hospitality. Tomorrow, you will take the young warriors to the spot and follow the panther's trail. Bring back its pelt and we will honor your friend."

Kennedy passed at sunset, as though the vanishing orange sun took his soul with it as it descended over the horizon. I purchased some small bit of land from Bhekizizwe outside the village and we buried him, marking the grave with a wooden cross. We could not carry his body back to Natal. A week in the African heat would not allow it. I packed his belongings to eventually send back to his family in Texas by way of Sir Henry in England.

As dawn broke, all the young men of the village showed up armed with assegais. We took the wagons back to the stone ridge, found the remains of the kudu Kennedy had killed, or what little the scavengers had left, and set out over the ridge. On the far side, we formed a line to descend and enter the grassland to search for tracks or any other sign of the panther. One local warrior found a print that led to others. He led the way for the rest of us, some men spreading out in case the tracks were lost or the panther doubled back. By mid day the spoor was lost in the midst of those of an antelope herd. Try as we could, the panther tracks could not be found again.

We headed back to the wagons while we still had sunlight. Along the way, I heard whispers among the men from the village. Even some of our own people grumbled. The local villagers questioned our men, and they became even more agitated.

"Macumazahn," Mnqoba said as he walked beside me, "they do not like this. They each say those were not panther tracks. A big cat maybe, but not a panther. Many are saying it was a devil or *tokoloshe*, and I tend to agree."

"There was nothing supernatural about that beast, Mnqoba," I said.

"It was no ordinary cat. You must admit that. It stood on hind legs."

"Yes, but it was some kind of cat, not a devil. An aberration."

"Your father had taught me much about God, Macumazahn, and some little about the devil. Satan is a powerful demon to be feared. Perhaps he has power to change what Unkulunkulu has created and make this abomination, to do its bidding, as witch doctors do with the *tokoloshe*. Therefore, it is a devil."

"Mnqoba," I said tightly, trying to curb my frustration, "abnormalities occur naturally. Like a cow with two heads or an extra limb."

"Yes, and they are always put to death because of devils."

I shook my head and ended the conversation.

When we returned to the kraal at dusk, many of the warriors sought out the witch doctor. They surrounded him and began talking at once in hushed tones that Mnqoba and I could not overhear, but they cast us suspicious looks while we unleashed the oxen to feed and water them. Presently the *inyanga* motioned them to quiet, then pointed from one to another to state their concerns. After they had spoken to his satisfaction, he walked away, trailed by the warriors.

Presently, a warrior came to us and told us Bhekizizwe demanded our presence.

Under escort, we returned to the palatial hut. Illuminated by a large fire, Bhekizizwe sat upon his stool, surrounded by half a dozen warriors with stoic features and the old *inyanga*, who appeared nervous.

"Macumazahn," the chief began, "you did not catch this killer panther."

"No, Great Bhekizizwe," I said.

"Is it truly a panther you seek, a panther that killed the man you buried?"

I glanced at Mnqoba, whose brow was furrowed and his lips tight in a straight line. He suspected where these questions were leading.

"Yes, Bhekizizwe," I said, which set off some of his warriors behind us into mumbling among themselves. The *inyanga* straightened his old body and raised his chin. "But also not a panther," I hastened to say. "It was a beast unlike any I have ever seen. Deformed. Larger than an ordinary panther. Perhaps its parent bred with something else. However, it was something akin to a panther. A large black cat that is a man-killer."

"Word has spread from your own men that it walked upright, as a man," Bhekizizwe said.

I noticed Mnqoba's eyes narrow. It did not come from him, but probably the man who was with us when Kennedy was attacked, the one I had sent to hurry the wagons along.

"It did briefly, Bhekizizwe," I said.

"I saw the wounds," the witch doctor said. "They were not panther wounds."

"This is no panther, Macumazahn," the chief declared.

"It is a demon," the *inyanga* said.

"I am not aware that demons or devils take the form of panthers," I said.

"It must be a *tokoloshe*," the inyanga said. "Another witch doctor has set it upon the land to devour our people and bring illness. Perhaps the *tokoloshe* was sent after you, Macumazahn, or the dead white man."

"You have brought a curse upon us, Macumazahn," Bhekizizwe said. "You must leave."

"The grave of the white man must be purified," the witch doctor said. "It was he the *tokoloshe* killed."

Bhekizizwe turned to him. "Should the body be dug up and sent away or destroyed?"

"Nay," the *inyanga* said. "That is not necessary. We shall gather as much salt as we can find and cover the grave with it. Then I must chant over it for two days to drive away the *tokoloshe*."

"Bhekizizwe," I said, "this was not a supernatural creature but an animal. We couldn't find it, but we followed its spoor far from your kraal. It has gone from the area and will not bother your people."

"The *tokoloshe* can appear again wherever it wants," the witch doctor said. "It will follow the one it killed. It will follow you, Macumazahn, who hunts it. Very bad for Bhekizizwe's people."

"You will leave when the sun rises," Bhekizizwe said. "And you will leave half your oxen as payment to the *inyanga* for fighting this curse you brought to our village. And any kills that you made. And half of your supplies."

I clenched my jaw at this outrage but remained calm, considering we were surrounded by armed and very superstitious Zulu. "Very well. And the wagon those oxen pull?"

"We have no need for a wagon," Bhekizizwe said, then rubbed his chin thoughtfully. "But we will use its wood for cooking fires and the metal bits to fashion tools. The other wagon you may keep, Macumazahn."

"Bhekizizwe is too generous," I said with a bow, "as well as wise."

Bhekizizwe smiled at this. "Stay the night, Macumazahn. But you and your men will be gone from our kraal before the sun has risen. And do not return here, for this curse will follow you."

He stood up and walked into his hut.

"Shall we continue to hunt the devil cat?" Mnqoba asked as we returned to our wagons.

"No," I said. "Thanks to Bhekizizwe our supplies are now cut by half.

We will have one wagon and at least we can keep the horses, but trying to pick up the cat's trail would take too long and exhaust what we have. It's wounded and may die on its own. In any case, it was moving north and probably won't be back in this area again. Without Kennedy our trip is over. I have no desire to trophy hunt. Bhekizizwe has allowed us to keep one wagon, so we can get our men and what's left of our supplies back to Natal. Once we reach Maritzburg, I'll sell the remaining wagon and ride back to Durban on horseback. You, Mnqoba, may have the other horse if you wish, or sell it as part of your pay."

He shrugged. "What does a Zulu need with a horse? But I shall come back to Durban with you, Macumazahn, if just to make certain the curse does not follow you."

CHAPTER THREE

In Maritzburg we sold the oxen and wagon and paid off our men. I informed the British authorities of Kennedy's death and spent two days making the same statements over and over to a variety of bureaucrats until they were satisfied. I left his belongings with them to be sent on to Sir Henry and eventually to whatever family he had in America.

Mnqoba rode with me to Durban on the coast, all the while expositing on the supernatural nature of the beast that had killed Kennedy. He calmly refused to go his own way, insisting that he must stay with me so that the curse does not bring the devil cat upon me. Besides, he had a cousin in Durban.

"You should speak to the Opener of Roads," he said.

"I will certainly not," I said, recalling the last time I had seen the dwarf Zikali, at the end of the Zulu War. He had manipulated my friends and myself for his own gain to bring about the downfall of the house of Senzangakhona in revenge for Chaka killing his wives and children long ago. Besides, his home in the Black Kloof was some distance and I was tired of traveling.

"He is wise in the ways of spirits. He would be able to see this devil that follows you."

"The only devil following me is you!" I snapped.

After which he remained quiet until we reached Durban.

We immediately went to my small house, which seemed even smaller than ever and could hide in any corner of the Grange, my home in Yorkshire, and go without notice, yet it felt cozy and familiar. Mnqoba took charge of the horses, and would stay with cousins not far away.

"If you will not visit the Opener of Roads," he said as he led the exhausted horses toward a nearby stable, "then I shall seek an *isangoma* to intervene for your sake."

"Don't bother," I called after him.

I thought nothing more of his superstitious comment as I stored my belongings, cleaned myself, and prepared for bed. The sun had yet to set, but I was exhausted. Although less than a year had passed since Captain Good, Sir Henry, and I had gone to the land of the Kukuanas and come back, I seemed ages older and tired too easily of traveling. I was asleep before my head dropped onto the pillow.

Some time in the middle of the night, a noise in the other room disturbed me, rousing me from sleep. Believing it was Mnqoba, I tugged on a pair of trousers and padded out of the tiny bedroom to demand what he was doing at such an hour. The dark shape that met me was not the tall, narrow form of Mnqoba but the smooth figure of a woman.

My mind was still muddled by sleep and I thought of someone who had died many years ago, the beautiful but evil woman who had been a catalyst Zikali had used to bring about the downfall of an empire. Why I would suddenly think of Mameena, I do not know. She had not been on my mind for a long time, though her apparition seemed to haunt me.

In the gloom I found a candle and struck a match to light it.

The figure was no specter, as I feared, but solid and natural.

"Who are you?" I demanded. "What are you doing here?"

She turned and faced me with a graceful movement. In the moment I was reminded of the witch Nombe, who was a great-granddaughter of Zikali and had met a tragic end brought about by her own jealousies. She had been young and beautiful. This woman was a little older, but no less handsome. The faint candlelight sent shadows across a smooth copper face framed by long wavy curls. The figure ineffectually hidden under a wrap of red cloth was no different from a woman decades younger.

She took time to size me up with her dark eyes that seemed to twinkle in the light from the candle. Her bearing was unapologetic, almost regal, as she stood in my living room, unannounced and uninvited. A small smile tugged at the corner of her lips.

Frustrated, I located a lantern and lighted the wick, bringing a brighter light into the small room. I set the lantern on the table beside me and puffed out the candle. Facing her again, I was struck by her beauty. She may have been in her forties, but she looked at least a decade younger.

"I said, who are you?" I tried to cling to my evaporating anger out of sheer pride.

"I heard you the first time," she said in lightly accented English. "I am Izula."

"What are you doing here? How did you get in?"

"You do not lock your door, Macumazahn. As for why I am here, you sent for me."

"I did not!"

"Well," she said, walking around the room and looking at the bare walls and selves, "perhaps not you, but your spirit. I am here in answer to the call of your spirit."

"I think you should leave now," I said, considering returning to the bedroom to retrieve my pistol from its holster at my bedside.

"If it will make you feel more comfortable, you may get one of your guns. If you see me as a threat."

"I see you as a lunatic," I said, wondering if she really did read my mind or just my intentions from my expressions.

She smiled, causing her copper colored face to radiate. "Perhaps. I am a talker with spirits."

"An *isangoma*," I said. It was becoming clear, as I remembered Mnqoba's parting words. "Mnqoba brought you here, then. Where is he?"

She shrugged innocently. "Probably asleep at his cousin's home. *You* brought me, Macumazahn. Your spirit, at least."

"You don't look like an *isangoma*," I said, for she did not wear the traditional garb of a witch doctress, with the accompanying beads and skin bags of medicines. She wore only the red garment wrapped tightly around her and hide sandals on delicate feet.

She drew close to me, her eyes even with mine. "Perhaps I am not *isangoma*. Perhaps I am just a spirit, haunting you."

I reached out a touched her bare arm, feeling the cool smooth skin. "You are solid enough."

"Tell me, Macumazahn, where is the little carving Zikali gave you of the one who passed into darkness?"

I stepped back, surprised she would even know about the statue that resembled Mameena. I had packed it away and shipped it to England when I had moved at Sir Henry's request after our adventures in Kukuanaland. It stood on a shelf in my den.

"You know Zikali," I said, pieces to a different puzzle falling into place. "He sent you."

"I have never met Zikali in body, though we have often communicated in spirit. He is my great-great grandfather. As with Nombe, whom you knew."

"Chaka murdered his wives and children," I said, "which was the reason for his revenge on the Zulu royal house. How can you be his great-great granddaughter?"

"Chaka did not kill all the children. Zikali was very … active … in his youth, despite his ugliness. Nombe's great grandmother had escaped, so why wouldn't mine?"

"Where did you learn to speak English so well?" I asked.

"I was schooled in England. My mother was a servant to one of your lords. When I began to speak with the spirits, she sent me back to Cape Colony. The English might have locked me away. They don't seem to understand spirits very well."

"So Zikali trained you to be an *isangoma*?"

"I told you that I have never met Zikali. I have never been to the Black Kloof. And even though we have spoken in dreams, he did not send me. You did, Macumazahn."

"I didn't send for you. We've never met, and until minutes ago I had no idea of your existence. Now please go away."

"No," she said is Zulu. "It was your spirit that called to me, Watcher-by-Night. I have come to answer your question."

"Question? What question?"

"As to whether the thing that you saw was natural or supernatural, devil or creature."

My face heated as I thought of the strange panther that had stood on hind legs. It had been Mnqoba who claimed it was a devil, not I, for I believed it was some animal either never before seen or a victim of deformities. Mnqoba had planted a seed in my mind that made me doubt ever so slightly my resolve as to its origin. The only way she would know of the creature would be through Mnqoba.

"Then Mnqoba did send you," I insisted.

She sighed and dropped into one of the wicker chairs. "I already told you. How many times must I explain." She crossed her long legs, the red fabric falling aside to reveal smooth bronze skin.

"Okay," I said, waving dismissive hands. I sank into the chair opposite her. "All right, for the sake of argument I will agree that neither Zikali nor

Mnqoba sent you. What is it you want?"

"To ease your mind," she said, smiling. "Or to make it more troubled," she added, her smile vanishing.

"Which?" I asked.

"That is entirely up to you, Macumazahn. I will tell you the truth, that there is nothing supernatural at work. You are not cursed, and a devil did not kill that American."

"Then what was it?"

She smiled and leaned forward, close enough that I could smell a fresh flowery scent drifting from her. "Ah, so now you believe in what I say. Now you actually seek my council. But, alas, I cannot say more. I am a speaker to spirits, not to the strange things of this world. What it is, you must discover. I can only tell you what it is not."

I sat back, folding my arms over my chest. "I am done with the affair. I wounded the beast and it will probably die of its injuries, if it hasn't done so already. I will be leaving Natal very soon."

Her features became very serious, a few years added in the glow of the lantern. "No, you will not. Not yet. Your work here is unfinished."

"Don't be ridiculous. I came back for a hunting trip, and my partner is now dead. I'll be settling matters as to the disposition of this house, and then I'm on the next boat back to England. I have no more work here. In fact, I needn't work for the rest of my life."

"Your duty, then," she said. "Your obligation. Africa will not let you go. Not yet and not for long."

"More talk of spirits?"

"Yes. Your spirit is tied to the soil of Africa."

"Well, I have nothing more to do with the present situation."

"Yes you do."

"What makes you think so?" I demanded, jumping to my feet and standing over her.

She rose slowly and reached out and stroked the beard along my cheek with the tips of her fingers, her eyes gazing into mine with sympathy. My anger instantly vanished. "Because, my dear Macumazahn, although this thing is not supernatural, yet there are spirits who call. A great evil is moving, and the spirits mourn. They cry out for help. If you calm yourself you will hear them. They call one name. *Macumazahn*."

"What evil?" I asked.

"Who may say? It is a dark cloud that grows. You can bring light to it. Or perhaps it will engulf you and all our people."

"You give a lot of hope," I said sarcastically.

"No, it is you who must bring the hope. You have much to do, Macumazahn. And I must leave you." She glided toward the door in easy, fluid movements.

"Will I see you again," I asked, then regretted the question as to how it sounded.

"That depends on you, Macumazahn. It is your spirit that calls to me."

She opened the door to the cool night.

"Oh, and tell Mnqoba," she said, "that I am sorry."

"Sorry for what?"

But she was already gone, the night swallowing her up as though she had never been there, as though she were not the solid form I had thought she was.

Izula was an intriguing woman. Whether she could actually communicate with spirits was debatable and I could not believe in it. In my dealing with Zikali, the dwarf wizard of the Black Kloof, I had witnessed some bizarre events and I had seen him trick and manipulate people, including me, although he had also given me knowledge of future events that tended to weaken my skepticism. Despite what Izula said, my business in this matter was finished.

Or so I thought.

Early the next morning, someone pounded on my door. Upon opening it, I found an Englishman in a crisp linen suit and an expensive white straw hat. He was in his thirties, with the bland face of a bureaucrat.

"Mr. Quatermain, I am Elliot Mortimer, with the Colonial Office. I need to ask you some questions about the death of Jacob Kennedy."

I invited him to sit on the veranda where there was at least a breeze dispelling some of the heat.

"I've given official statements," I said. "Several times, in fact. I was assured all legal issues were covered."

"Of course. My office did receive copies. We just want to corroborate your statement and make sure there were no details left out."

And so I described the events of Kennedy's death, leaving out, as I had in the official statements, the unusual aspects of the panther in question.

"You wounded the animal," he said.

"It was a difficult shot. The cat was on top of Mr. Kennedy and moving

"You wounded the animal."

very quickly, and I had little time for a perfect aim. I tried for the head but only hit the shoulder. The rest of the body was not in my view."

"I understand. Your reputation as a hunter is exceptional. You tracked the animal but never encountered it up close?"

"No," I said, lying as I had to the other officials.

"Nothing unusual about the cat?"

"Like what?" I asked. What was unusual was a question such as that, as though he expected me to answer that it was some strange monster that walked upright.

"Oh, as in size or coloration," he said, his eyes flicking away from me.

"It was a panther. A black leopard. Nothing to its coloration except black."

"Nothing strange about the tracks you followed?"

"We lost them in an antelope heard, unable to follow them further. The men of the Bhekizizwe kraal helped in the hunt. They are aware of the animal being nearby, but it probably moved north from there, if it survived. I know of a couple of kraals in that direction. Perhaps you should send word to them to watch out for a wounded cat."

Mortimer shook his head with a quick dismissal. "Oh, don't concern yourself with the matter any more, Mr. Quatermain. We're looking into it to make certain no one else is injured. I doubt we'll ever find the carcass, or even hear of the man-eater again. Will you be returning to the bush on another hunt?"

"No," I said. "We were scheduled to be gone for two months, but I may book passage back to England soon."

"Well," he said, getting to his feet, "if there is anything our office can do, please let us know. I'm certain you are anxious to return to England. All this affair with Mr. Kennedy is at an end, so don't concern yourself with it any more. Tragic though it is. But then, this is Africa. A very dangerous place, as you well know."

He left me feeling even more uncomfortable than my visit from Izula.

I watched him walk away, his hands thrust into his pockets. He passed two men loitering on a corner, their hats shadowing their faces. Mortimer slowed down and seemed to speak briefly to them. One of the men nodded as Mortimer passed by and quickened his pace again. The two remained, smoking cigarettes and looking as though they were in mild conversation with each other, but neither actually spoke. They were rough looking men, the type who would have once been soldiers but never rising in the ranks. Their clothes were worn and wrinkled, in need of a wash. Their broad brim felt hats bore heavy sweat stains. One man's hat bore a zebra pelt as a band.

I have seen men like these many times, for they thought their strength and arrogance could win them fame and fortune in Africa, where they just gained an early grave. I watched them intently, while casually smoking my pipe, as I have watched game upon a hunt. They were two hundred yards away, standing in the hot sun, trying not to appear to be looking in my direction. They became increasingly uncomfortable, by the continuous shifting movements and the anxious puffs on their cigarettes. Eventually, one motioned to the other, and they walked off. Did they leave because of the heat, or had I made them nervous?

CHAPTER FOUR

Izula's words ate at me. Not so much her talk about spirits or evil, but that it concerned me in particular. I am not one to bring hope, as she had said. My life has been filled with tragedies, as with most people. I have buried two dear wives and many good friends, both white and black. I am no missionary as my father had been to offer hope, nor am I a brave man. But I was responsible for allowing a wounded predator to wander free, and if one person dies under its claws, that is upon me. How could I find one cat among the wilds of Africa? Stranger things have happened, for I had found a childhood friend after many years of separation, and she became my wife for too short a time, though leaving me with a fine son, the joy of my life. What ever created that strange cat, I had no part in it. It had killed Kennedy, through no fault of mine. But my shot had missed killing it and it might still be alive and a danger to others. That was my responsibility.

I told no one of my leaving. I went south to visit an old acquaintance, surreptitiously picking up a few supplies. Then in the night I headed north where I could purchase a wagon and team, paying extra so that the merchants would lose the transaction and forget my face.

Loading supplies for an extended expedition, I turned to find the tall, lean figure of Mnqoba standing over me. He wore his same threadbare trousers, dirty blue shirt, and no shoes.

"What are you doing here?" I demanded.

"My cousin Owethu told me that you left Durban. I went to Maritzberg where you had sold your last wagon, but my cousin Zibuyile told me that you have not been there, so I came here, where my cousin Jabulane told me he saw you on the road."

"What do you want?" I asked as I secured the last crate.

"I will go with you."

"No. I go alone."

"Did you visit the Opener of Roads? Did he say you must go?"

"No. I haven't seen Zikali. It's just something I have to do."

"To hunt down the devil panther."

"I wounded it, it's my responsibility."

"And you are my responsibility, Macumazahn. I will come to watch over you."

Izula's words concerning Mnqoba sprang to my mind. Were they prophetic?

"I don't need you," I said, trying to sound sharp but unable to feel anger toward the man.

Mnqoba smiled. "No, you don't." And he began hitching the oxen to the wagon.

No further word was spoken. Once the team was hitched, I climbed onto the wagon. Mnqoba led the oxen through the town, then climbed onto the box beside me when the vast stretch of veldt opened out for us.

The days were uneventful. We traveled, stopping at night, shooting the occasional game for a meal of fresh meat, though little was needed since there were only two of us. We rode in silence most of the time, and I enjoyed the quiet and the vastness of the African hills and grasslands. It was good to be back in the land of my youth, away from the cold damp of England, to feel the African sun burning into my skin. To breathe the air filled with fragrant blossoms, musty decay, and the occasional reminder of animal herds.

We passed antelope and wildebeest, dozens of elephants, and zebra. I had hunted these most of my life, but hunting had been a vocation, a way to earn a living, and I was good at it. Now I could hunt only for food, if necessary, and allow these wonderful animals to roam unmolested and admire their beauty.

Upon the third day I noticed the men following us.

"They hold back," Mnqoba said. "So that they do not overtake us."

"Yes. What do you make out? Two men on horseback?"

"Yes, Macumazahn."

"They don't know what they're doing, do they? They're trying to keep us in sight, but don't realize we can see them. They don't use a fire at night, to hide from us. Which should make it very uncomfortable for sleeping. One would need to stay awake at all times. I'm sure they are miserable after a couple of days of this."

"They follow us?"

"Yes."

"Why, Macumazahn?"

"I don't know. Two men were watching my house after a colonial government man paid me a visit to make sure I would not do exactly what I am now doing. He seemed anxious for me to return to England."

"You think these two are the same men?"

"Maybe they're just keeping an eye on me for the government, although I don't know why."

He glanced at the western horizon. "Another hour and the sun will set and we will camp. I will get out and hide behind a mimosa tree until it gets very dark, then I will sneak up upon them. I will see who they are and hear them plot, then come to you."

"Too dangerous, Mnqoba. I'll do it while you continue and make camp."

"No, Macumazahn. You are a great hunter, greater than any in Africa, but I am stealthy and I am black."

"What does your color have to do with it?" I demanded.

"I cannot be seen in the dark. Although you are very dark for a white man, you stand out. Especially with your English clothes." He grinned at me.

I couldn't fault his logic.

As the sun began to set, I guided the oxen toward one lone mimosa tree. Mnqoba stripped off his shirt and trousers, leaving only his breeches. He slipped off the wagon, dropped to the ground, and sat in the shade of the tree, his back against its trunk, while I continued on for half a mile.

I kept looking back, through the wagon, but his dark skin became invisible in the growing shadows.

I set up camp by myself for the first time since we had begun, feeling the heavy loneliness, even though Mnqoba was less than a mile behind me.

I built the fire, made a meal of biltong, dried game meat, and canned beans, and waited. I started at every sound, anxious for Mnqoba's return. If these were the same two men following us as I had seen in Durban, then I didn't like them. They were unsavory looking and dangerous.

There came a chirp that could have been a small animal or bird, but unlike anything on the veldt.

"Mnqoba?" I whispered.

"It is I, Macumazahn," he said, stepping into the firelight. "I did not want you to shoot me."

I handed him some biltong and he sat down next to me.

"What did you see?" I asked.

"I waited by the tree until dark, then waited longer to be sure, then I walked toward the camp of the strangers. I could not see very much, but they are noisy people, these white men. They think they are stealthy, but they are ignorant. So I followed my ears. Presently, they built a very small fire hidden behind a tree. They cooked coffee and canned food. They are armed with revolvers and rifles, but not very good ones if they plan to hunt. They sat so they could see the glow of the fire you had set, Macumazahn. But they did not speak. I drew close enough to hear them, but they said nothing. Even when they heard a rodent scurry, and drew their guns, they did not say anything. When one went to sleep while the other watched, I left."

"What did they look like?"

He shrugged. "White men."

"That's not very helpful. Did one wear a hat with a zebra pelt?"

"Yes, Macumazahn."

"Then it must be the same two men from Durban."

"Do you want me to sneak back to their camp and kill them?"

"No, of course not."

"If we leave during the night …"

"They will follow our trail and catch up to us."

"I could free the horses," Mnqoba said.

"And strand them out here?"

He shrugged, unconcerned over their fate. "They have supplies carried by a pack mule. They will not starve. They will just have to walk. We have done worse on many of our travels."

I remembered many of my own experiences on foot in the wilds of Africa. Walking across deserts with no water. Finding little or no game, barely surviving on dried meat. I would not want to repeat any of that. But game was plentiful in this area, as was water. Perhaps without horses they would be forced to return, and by the time they came back, our trail would be swept away.

"Yes, Mnqoba, set their horses free. As long as you aren't in danger of getting shot."

"It is simple enough. They have them tethered to a mimosa. I can cut them free and be back in no time."

"Let's hook up the oxen first," I said, "then we can leave as soon as you come back, before sunrise."

"This is a great trick we play on these men. But are you certain you do not want me to kill them?"

"No. I don't like that they're following us, but they could be working for the colonial man, Mortimer. Why should they be sneaking about if they work for the government?"

"They have the smell of paid soldiers. I do not like them. It is best they are not behind us to sneak up at night and cut our throats."

"Setting their horses free will slow them down."

Mnqoba set out an hour later after we had hooked up the oxen to the wagon. I loaded what few articles we had removed for our camp, then sat on the back of the wagon to await the Zulu's return. The fire began to die down. We hadn't added fuel to it, and I had no desire to keep it burning after we left, lest we set the grass on fire.

After a time, I heard shouts. It was too far and too dark to see anything, but the sounds conjured images from my imagination. There were angry cries, horses hooves pounding the hard packed earth, then pistol fire. Then more confused shouts punctuated by some colorful language.

Presently I heard the soft padding of running bare feet.

Mnqoba's grinning face appeared out of the darkness.

I hurriedly kicked dirt into the fire, burying the last bits of embers, then climbed to the front of the wagon and started the team forward, the wheels turning as Mnqoba leapt to the box beside me. He laughed hysterically for a time and I could not get a word out of him until we were at least a mile away from our camp. I was worried the men would run after him and use their rifles against us, and told him so, but he waved away my concerns while doubled over in laughter.

"No, Macumazahn," he said eventually, calming down. "That would have been very uncomfortable for them. They needed to climb the mimosa tree first."

"Why?"

"When I returned to their camp, the watcher had fallen asleep. As some white men are prone to do, they had removed their boots for the night. I simply walked up to them, took their boots, tied them together, and tossed them into the higher branches of the mimosa. Then I cut the tethers for the horses and pack mule. When the watcher awoke, his shouts frightened the animals. His shots frightened them even more. They are probably many miles away by now."

"He could have shot you, Mnqoba."

"Nay, Macumazahn. I kept the mimosa between us. He never even saw me. Although I feared that they would believe we chased away their mounts and that they would hurry after us with their rifles, so I decided to make it difficult for them to follow on foot. Therefore my plan of stealing their boots. But I could not strand them on the veldt, as you said, therefore I put them high in the tree. White men do not like to run barefoot. Their feet are too pale and soft."

He stretched out his own feet with their hard callused soles and wiggled his dusty toes.

He laughed so hard I was certain our two shadows could hear him back at their camp site.

We returned to the area near where we had lost Kennedy. I had no hope of finding a trail from the killer panther, but we took a day and searched. I would have returned to the kraal of Bhekizizwe to learn if anything new had been discovered, but I decided to avoid the village. We had not parted on very good terms. But I knew of other kraals north and east of Bhekizizwe, and the panther had been moving north and slightly east when we last sighted its tracks. After taking the day to fruitlessly search for track, and making certain we did not have anyone following, we camped for the night, then set off to the nearest kraal to the east.

"This is the kraal of Umgibeli," Mnqoba said. "I have never been here, but I have a cousin who took a wife from this kraal. Very pretty girl. Maybe there are other pretty girls here."

As we approached the cluster of huts surrounded by the wall of thorn logs, several warriors armed with assegais came out and formed a line, preventing us from entering.

"I wouldn't count on marrying anyone from this kraal quite yet," I told him. "They don't look particularly friendly toward us."

"And I will not mention my cousin, either. He is not a likeable man. He may have stolen the girl from here. Besides, I have no cattle to offer in exchange for a wife."

I brought the oxen to a halt in front of the line of warriors. They did not make any aggressive movements, nor did I reach for either my holstered revolver or my rifle.

Mnqoba stood up on the box and waved his own assegai, which, once in his trousers and shirt, was the only thing that made him look Zulu.

"Greetings men of Umgibeli. I am Mnqoba of the Zulu, son of Ulaqoba. This is the friend of the Zulu, who is called Macumazahn, Watch-by-Night. We come to seek help and to offer gifts."

The warriors stirred, some losing their cold, stoic expressions and glancing questioningly at one another. A number murmured a word: *Macumazahn.*

One warrior went through the gateway and into the kraal while the others maintained the line and did not reply to Mnqoba. Presently, the man returned, motioned to his comrades, and the line parted to reveal the gate in the outer wall. As I drove the oxen into the kraal, the warriors flanked us. Two men on either side took hold of the harness for the lead oxen and guided them. Two others walked behind the wagon, peering inside. We were brought to a halt, and the head warrior motioned to us with his assegai.

Mnqoba and I were escorted to the largest hut, where a stocky older man sat upon a stool. His heavy arms were folded over his great chest and the warriors flanking him appeared ready to hurl their assegais at his command.

"Greetings great Umgibeli," I said.

"You are Macumazahn?" he asked, eyeing me up and down.

I am not an intimidating person. I am short, tend toward the thin side, and walk with a slight limp. I was also more than halfway through my fifth decade.

"Yes, Umgibeli."

He looked at Mnqoba, who nodded.

"Why do you come here? White men who come into our country usually bring trouble. What do you bring, Macumazahn?"

"We are hunting, Umgibeli."

"Is this Zulu your servant?"

"No. Mnqoba is my friend."

"White men do not make friends with black men," the chief said.

"Macumazahn does," Mnqoba said. "Have you not heard of Macumazahn?"

Umgibeli inclined his head in acknowledgement. "I have heard."

"Besides," Mnqoba continued, "he pays me well to help him on his hunts."

"Why hunt here?" Umgibeli asked. "Game is more plentiful to the south. Why not stay there and hunt?"

"Because we hunt a particular animal, a large panther," I said.

Umgibeli's brow rose just a fraction. Two of the warriors behind him widened their eyes.

"So you know what I mean," I said.

"A large black panther," the chief said. "As large as a man."

"Yes," I said.

"A panther devil," Mnqoba said, and I glared at him.

"This panther has been cursed," Umgibeli said, as though agreeing with him. "Do you have magic to drive it away?"

"Have you or your people seen it?" I asked.

"Yes. It has killed some of our cattle. It has fought our warriors. It is a demon that can walk like a man and kill like a beast. Do you have magic against it, Macumazahn?"

"I have my rifle," I said. "I faced it before, but it escaped. It killed another white man who was in my care. I am hunting it down so that it will not kill again."

Umgibeli nodded slowly. "Even if it kills only black men?"

"I want no one to die because of it, white or black."

"Do you have magic in your rifle, that you can kill demons?"

"It is flesh and blood. A bullet will kill it."

He nodded again. "You may stay in our country for a time, and we shall see."

"Thank you, Umgibeli. Can one of your people show us where it was last seen?"

"At daylight. Then we shall see."

CHAPTER FIVE

They offered us a small hut for the night. I presented them with some gifts of rolls of cloth I had brought, which I have often used in trading. They still treated us with suspicion, but they accepted that we were there to help hunt down the creature that had been troubling them. It had taken one cow and three goats over the past week, the latest a goat very near the kraal only two days ago. Umgibeli feared that it was a matter of time before it took one of his people.

Despite their skepticism, they seemed anxious to have help in stopping the beast, or as they saw it, putting an end to the curse.

We joined the chief and his retinue in front of his hut for the evening meal. It was here he proudly displayed his daughters, only one whom was of marrying age and was a very pretty young woman. Umgibeli told me that no one in his village owned enough cattle to give in exchange for marriage. He kept hinting and inquiring how many cattle I had. I explained that I had many at my home very far away, across the Dark Waters, but that I was too old to marry again.

Mnqoba whispered to me, "I wish I had your cattle, Macumazahn. She is the most beautiful woman I have ever seen."

"She is quite lovely," I said. "Save up you cattle, my friend, and maybe we will return some day."

"Ah, but by then it will be too late. Someone else will marry her. Oh, what a fool I have been, not saving up and building a nice big herd that would make any chief proud. Instead I have wandered around, having adventures."

"You are still young, Mnqoba. There is time."

"I am no longer a young warrior and I have nothing to offer her. Alas."

Liyana, the chief's eldest, served us beverages from a gourd. She was the color of coffee, with delicate features, and probably in her late teens. She would have been married off sooner, but Umgibeli was probably holding out for the most cattle he could get in exchange. Her dark eyes were compassionate, and they often traveled to my companion, Mnqoba. He stared unabashedly at her, and she smiled coyly in return.

At dawn, Zakhele, one of Umgibeli's herdsmen, took us to the place under some mimosa trees where the last goat was killed. Even though the earth was dry and hard packed, there was no trace of the slaughter. Too many animals and people had trod over the ground since. The cattle had been driven along here to and from the kraal. The same was true of the other places Zakhele took us. The goats were attacked near the kraal, and one herdsman had been knocked down and raked with claws, though not killed after the goat was carried off. The cow had been killed further away, the rolling hills hiding the village.

Here, the herd was now grazing. Zakhele pointed to the spot where the cow had been killed and partially devoured. He had seen the beast himself and had chased it away. According to him, he bravely ran toward it, yelling. That is a ploy sometimes used to frighten away big cats. The cat will be startled enough to run off, but will return shortly once it realizes there is little threat. Zakhele had moved the herd to avoid the cat's return, leaving the cow's carcass to appease the devil. When he looked again later that day, most of the carcass was gone. Of course, there was nothing to see now, a week later.

Mnqoba and I wandered off, leaving the herd so that we might find tracks. Unfortunately, most of the ground was grazed upon each day and the cattle left their mark, obliterating all else. We found a rise that had not seen hoof prints for some days and had a good view of the countryside. The grazing herd on one side and the rolling veldt on the other.

At the crest of this hill, a squat mimosa offered meager shade. Mnqoba strode to it, shaded his eyes with one hand, and scanned the horizon.

I was under the impression that this was a hopeless task. To find a single beast in all of this wilderness. True, if it had a ready meal every time the villagers took the herds out of the kraal to graze, it might stay in the area. Unless it felt threatened.

"Macumazahn."

I turned to Mnqoba, but he was no longer looking at the veldt, rather at the ground at his feet. Walking to him, I followed his gaze. There, between his bare feet, were the remains of a cigarette.

I have seen the occasional pipe used at the village, though most preferred snuff. Umgibeli had his pipe after diner last night, and I had joined him with my own, sharing some of my tobacco with him, which he greatly enjoyed. But I had not seen any member of his tribe rolling and smoking a cigarette. Could our shadows from Durban have followed us this far?

"White man," Mnqoba said.

"How can you be certain?" I asked.

He reached down with the point of his assegai and shifted the butt, tossing it on the hard earth.

"It was stomped under a boot. Natives would crush it against a rock or tree, so that the grass does not catch fire."

"Boots aren't exclusively a white man's property," I pointed out.

"True, but I have not seen any black men out here wearing boots."

I agreed with him. "Do you think our friends caught up with us? They may have been able to find their horses and then follow our wagon tracks."

"No, Macumazahn. They would have come south of here. The actions of white men are sometimes irrational, but it does not seem likely that they circled Umgibeli's kraal by many miles merely to find shade under this mimosa and watch the herds graze. They were following us, or rather you, and so would be watching the kraal."

We went in search of Zakhele, finding him guiding the herd along.

"Zakhele, have you seen other white men around?" I asked.

"No, Macumazahn," he said. "Very few white men come through our country. As you know, there is better hunting south and east of us. No elephants around for ivory. I have not seen white men myself for many months. There was a kraal of Boers that way, many miles, but they were killed when I was small. Some argument with our people, I believe."

He had waved his hand in a vaguely north west direction.

"No one lives there now?" I asked.

"No, Macumazahn."

"How far away?"

He shrugged. "I have never been there. Maybe two days travel. It is close to the border with Transvaal. We stay away from it."

Mnqoba and I circled the grazing land of the herds in search of spoor, either man or predator, but found none. There were antelope and zebra, but nothing else and nothing recent. When we returned to Umgibeli's kraal for the evening, following behind the herds in case we might spot something attacking any stragglers, Umgibeli called for our attendance.

We enjoyed a simple meal with the chief, served by his daughters and younger wives.

Mnqoba sighed when Liyana appeared. The young woman glanced at him and favored him with a smile.

"Are you rich with cattle that you can make moon faces at my eldest?" Umgibeli demanded.

Mnqoba lowered his eyes. "No, great Umgibeli. I have no cattle and no home to call my own."

Umgibeli laughed. "A poor man with a great heart, friend Mnqoba. Were that you were rich; you would make a good husband for Liyana and a good son-in-law for me, for you are strong and intelligent and a friend to Macumazahn. But you are poor, so a marriage can never be. Alas, since no one else has come to offer me cattle for Liyana, you may still have time to gather a fortune, but do not waste that time, Mnqoba."

"Are there no other suitors?" Mnqoba asked with a spark of hope.

"Not in this kraal. Everyone in my kraal knows of Liyana's temper. She is too much like her mother. There were two suitors from the kraal north of us, but they have not come for some time. Three months at least. One had already pledged forty cows and one bull, but he has not returned. Perhaps he has found a better deal elsewhere. Owe!"

As she passed behind the chief, Liyana swung the gourd she was carrying and smacked her father on the back of the head. Then she stuck her tongue out at him.

"Speaking of other kraals," I said, hoping to change the subject and defuse a family squabble, "I understand that there was a Boer kraal nearby."

Umgibeli rubbed the back of his head, scowled at his retreating daughter, then shook his head. "No. Not for many years. When my father was chief, the Boers perpetrated some great evil and were all killed. My father may have had some hand in it, or it may have been the chief from the kraal nearer. I was very small at the time and it was never mentioned afterwards. I once saw the kraal when I was a young warrior on a hunt, but the huts were all empty and the crops were choked with grass. No one has lives there for many years."

"We saw signs of a white man nearby, where the cattle were grazing," I said.

"Then he was hidden, because I would have heard of a white man near our cattle. Macumazahn we trust, but no other white man. Did you not see any sign of the devil panther?"

"No. But that could also be good news. Perhaps it has moved on. Has this other kraal to the north been bothered by the panther?"

Umgibeli shook his head. "I know not, since it has been three months since I have heard from any of them. That is not unusual, as we may go a year before our people meet for one reason or another. Long ago, our people used to battle over land, until the Black One brought us together as Zulu." He referred to Chaka uniting the tribes, after defeating them in battles. Former kings are rarely mentioned by name, if it can be avoided.

"Perhaps I will pay a visit to this other kraal," I said. "Maybe they have seen the panther."

"Then you will take Zakhele with you," Umgibeli said. "He will carry a message to their chief, Izoqa, so that you are received as friends. Sometimes Izoqa is difficult to get along with. His eldest son is he who sought Liyana. He is far more agreeable than his father, but then he is young."

I accepted Zakhele as our guide and ambassador to the kraal of Izoqa, and bade Umgibeli and his family a good night.

Chapter Six

The trip to Izoqa's kraal over the rolling veldt was uneventful, and after three days we sighted the cluster of huts and kraals nestled in a shallow valley. It was such a peaceful place, with a stream running past the kraal, fields of corn growing high in the distance, and cattle dotting the grassland. On the wagon box beside Mnqoba, Zakhele stiffened. Even Mnqoba face drew a puzzled expression.

"Something is wrong," Mnqoba said.

"The cattle," Zakhele said. "They are scattered. No one is tending them."

I gave the reins to the oxen team to Mnqoba and reached behind me for my rifle. We rode into the kraal, Zakhele dropping to the ground and holding his assegai ready. No one came out to meet us. We went unchallenged.

There were no fires, no smell of cooking, no voices, except for an occasional bay of a goat or moo of a cow in the distance.

"Everyone is gone," Zakhele said in a hushed voice, refusing to go further. "This kraal is cursed."

"Nonsense," I said, dropping to the ground. "There is a logical explanation. Have you heard of any illness in the area? Fever?"

Zakhele shook his head.

Mnqoba took another one of the Winchesters from the wagon and joined me. He sniffed the air. "There is no scent of death, Macumazahn. All the people of Izoqa have vanished. The earth has swallowed them up."

I scowled at both men and their superstitions.

"Let's start searching the huts," I said. "Someone might still be left, or there might be some sign of what happened."

"And if a disease took them, would we not get it?" Mnqoba asked.

"If a disease took them all," I said, "there would be bodies."

"True," he said and headed for the first hut to the right.

I took the first on the left, while Zakhele waited at the wagon, jumping at each sound.

After the third empty hut, I heard a strange noise that sounded like a cat. On the other side of the empty cattle kraal, Mnqoba ducked out of a hut, stood still, and cocked his head.

"Macumazahn!" He motioned for me to join him.

Once I reached his side, we listened for the odd cry. It came again, and we followed it to a hut. I bent down, my leg aching with the effort, and poked the barrel of my rifle into the dark interior. Something stirred inside. I could see nothing and had no desire to walk, or rather crawl, into a trap.

"Who is there?" I asked in Zulu.

They stirred again, and then came the weakened cry once more.

I lowered my gun and tried to sound unthreatening. "Do not be afraid. We are here to help."

Mnqoba knelt beside me. "Who is there, Macumazahn?"

A faint voice called out from the far end of the hut. "Who are you?"

"I am Mnqoba, son of Ulaqoba, and this is Macumazahn, Watch-by-Night, friend to the Zulu. You are safe. Come out."

Whoever it was stirred and Mnqoba and I stepped back to allow them to crawl through the doorway and not feel threatened. Presently, a small, thin, old woman came out a stood in front of the hut. Her eyes were huge in a gaunt face. Her dry skin wrapped tight around her bones. In her emaciated arms she cradled an infant who uttered a feeble cry.

I took one look at the child and told Mnqoba, "Find the nearest cow and get some milk. They're both starving."

The old woman turned her head slowly to the hut behind her. "There is another."

"Hurry!" I said, slapping Mnqoba on the arm.

Off he ran, calling to Zakhele.

I slung my rifle over my shoulder and reached out to help the woman, for she barely had enough strength to stand. She pulled back, fear filling her eyes. Whether it was fear of a white man or just a stranger, it didn't matter. I uttered soothing words and approached slowly. Stiff with apprehension, she allowed me to guide her to a reed mat next to the hut.

"We will get you food," I said. "Is there anyone else here?"

She shook her head.

"What is your name?"

"Busisiwe." Her lips were dry and cracked and her throat croaked in trying to speak. I had a wooden canteen slung over my shoulder and brought it around and slipped off the strap to offer her a drink. She looked down at the baby, then took the canteen from me. She poured a few drops of water onto two fingers, then touched them to the infant's lips. After three times doing this, she finally took a drink herself.

"Can you tell me what happened?" I asked. "Where is everyone?"

"Spirits," she said, then swallowed several times and tried to clear her throat. "Spirits took them . . . one by one . . . in the night."

Mnqoba returned with Zakhele and a sloshing gourd of warm milk. The herdsman stared at the old woman for a moment, then found another smaller gourd, had Mnqoba pour some milk into it, then took the baby from Busisiwe. I crawled into the hut and searched through the gloom, my eyes taking time to grow accustomed to the dark interior. Eventually I found the second child, slightly older, but still an infant. Outside, we fed each of the fresh milk, a few drops at a time. When the weak children drifted off to sleep, Mnqoba started a fire while Zakhele went to the stream for fresh water. Then he gathered some vegetables into a metal pot to make a stew with some meat that we had from a kill the day before.

"Now tell us what happened, mother," I said.

Busisiwe buried her face in her hands and sobbed. "Gone! All gone."

"Izoqa, your chief?" I asked.

"Is there anyone else here?"

She looked up at me. "Dead. They found him dead first. The spirits killed him, for there was no mark upon him. If not spirits, then it was witchcraft. Our doctor could do nothing and did not know what happened. He was next. Dead outside his hut. No marks."

"Sounds like they might have been poisoned," I said, wondering if somehow their food or water had become contaminated. "How many others died?"

"None."

"Then where are they?"

"Gone."

"Where?"

She shrugged. "To wherever the spirits took them."

"Only the chief and the doctor died? What happened to everyone else?"

"They vanished. One by one. The first morning, Njabulo lamented that his wife was gone. She had been with child. They counted four missing, all pregnant women. The two days later, five. And so it happened all through the time of the moon until only I and the two children are left. The oldest and the youngest. And so we wait to be taken away. Or to die."

"You won't die yet," I promised. "As soon as your strength returns, we will take you and the babies to the kraal of Umgibeli. There you will be safe, and we'll try to find out what happened to the rest of your people."

Her narrow, gaunt face darkened into a scowl. "I tell you the spirits took them. White men do not understand. This kraal is cursed. If you take us to Umgibeli's kraal, it will become cursed. Do not be stupid in such matters, Macumazahn."

I left her in her indignation and went to Mnqoba and Zakhele as they prepared the meal.

"I have never been married," Mnqoba said, "let alone have a child. I do not have any idea how to care for them."

Zakhele stirred the pot on the fire. "Do not worry. I have three sons and a daughter. I will help in caring for them. If we had been another day coming, I do not think they would be alive. At least they would be too weak to travel. Let them eat and rest, and we should be able to leave in the morning."

"I would rather not stay the night," Mnqoba said, looking around at the empty huts. "This place is cursed."

"Now don't you start that, too, Mnqoba," I said. "Come with me and we'll round up some cows and bring them into the kraal. We can take them with us in order to have fresh milk for the babies."

Out on the grassland, Mnqoba set to chasing some of the cattle. Zakhele would have been more appropriate to use in bringing in some cows, but I wanted him to stay with the old woman and the infants. In that quarter he had more experience than either Mnqoba or I. It had been many years since my son Harry had been a baby. I left Mnqoba to wrangle the cattle while I circled the exterior of the kraal and studied the wooden posts used as fencing.

On the side opposite the gate, I found a worn patch in the grass. There had been a lot of foot traffic here, but either the weather had brushed away any trace of a print or it had been done by design. I approached the wall of logs along this worn area and leaned against them. They gave under pressure. In a moment I found a narrow handhold that had been hacked between two posts and pulled. Four logs, wedged tightly in place, came away from the others. They had been neatly sawn at ground level, dirt cleverly disguising their cuts. They fit snuggly with their mates and would never have been noticed under casual observation. I squeezed through and found myself behind some of the larger huts, probably once belonging to Izoqa and his family. So, once this back door was fashioned it would have been easy for someone to enter at night and kill the chief. Yet, they had left no wound on Izoqa. Poison, therefore. But how was that accomplished? Someone sneaking in and poisoning his food or water? To what end? And did they then kidnap four or five people each night and force them to silently climb through the hole in the kraal wall? Again, to what end?

It made no sense to me, any more than blaming spirits.

I joined Zakhele at his cooking pot just as he was spooning a small helping of stew into a wooden bowl for Busisiwe. He did a double take as I approached, glancing over his shoulder toward the gate of the kraal.

"I did not see you come back, Macumazahn."

"Someone cut a back door into the kraal," I said.

"Oh," he said.

After he handed the bowl to Busisiwe, I took him behind the huts and showed him the opening.

"Izoqa's people would not do this," he said.

"I didn't think so."

"Spirits would not need to do this," he said after lengthy contemplation.

"No, they wouldn't."

"The devil cats?" he asked.

"Not very likely. Unless they learned to use tools. These logs were sawn off."

"Who, then?"

"I don't know. We'll take the old woman back to Umgibeli's kraal and tell your chief what we have found. Maybe he will gather warriors for us to return and search for the missing people."

Zakhele nodded.

As we walked back to the cooking fire, he said, "I still think this place is cursed."

CHAPTER SEVEN

The return trip to the kraal of Umgibeli took longer since we now had passengers whose delicate conditions required us to move slower, find less uneven ground, and stop often. We also brought some of Izoqa's cows with us to provide fresh milk for the infants. Zakhele drove the cattle and oversaw the nursing of Busisiwe and the children. The old woman revived with proper food and took charge of the babes herself, though she did not turn down Zakhele's help since they were a handful.

It was with weary hearts that we finally saw Umgibeli's kraal nestled among the rolling hills of the veldt.

A call went up within the kraal when we came into sight. A regiment of warriors, assegais raised, took formation outside the gate and looked even less friendly when Mnqoba and I had first arrived.

"They do not look pleased to see us," Mnqoba said beside me on the wagon box.

"No, they don't," I replied.

Zakhele pushed his way to the front of the half dozen cattle he had been driving and lifted his hand in salute.

"It is I, Zakhele!"

The warriors murmured some reply, but they still did not open their ranks to allow us entry into the kraal until we were close enough for them to see all our faces and that we were not ready to take arms against them. Zakhele they greeted somberly and they cast suspicious eyes at Mnqoba and me.

"What has happened, my brothers?" Zakhele asked as he helped guide our oxen into the kraal.

"Woe upon us, Zakhele," the leader of the warriors said. "Umgibeli, our chief, is dead. A curse has fallen upon our people. The spirits walk at night."

Mnqoba moaned. I shoved the reins into his hand and jumped off the wagon.

"What happened?" I demanded. "How did he die?"

The warrior did not hide his distrust. "He died from no wound, Macumazahn, six days ago. A curse took him. The witch doctor could not find any cause for his death, so he said the devils you hunt have taken revenge on him. It was your fault, Macumazahn, for coming here and seeking the devil cats."

"Macumazahn did not bring the devils," Zakhele said. "They were here before he came. Remember the cow and goats they took? Besides, the same death happened to Izoqa many days before. We found the kraal of Izoqa empty except for an old woman and two children."

The warriors crowded closer.

"They were all gone?" asked their captain.

"Yes. And the old woman told us of the deaths of Izoqa and their doctor," Zakhele said.

"What curse darkens our land?" the captain demanded. "After Umgibeli died, members of his house vanished. Then our doctor died in the same manner as our chief, and others vanished. Women who were with child. Will the spirits take all of us, as they carried away the people of Izoqa?"

"They weren't spirits," I said.

Mnqoba abandoned his job of leading the oxen away and hurried to the captain. "Umgibeli's house, you say? Gone? What of Liyana, the chief's daughter? Surely she has not vanished."

The captain glared at Mnqoba for an instant for his interruption, then cast his eyes to the ground and nodded. "Yes. Two days after the chief had died. With her three sisters. Then the doctor died. After that, three woman who were pregnant."

Mnqoba pulled on my arm. "Macumazahn! We must find them, even if it is to the land of the spirits that we must go."

"If Zakhele is right," the captain said, "we need only wait until the spirits come for each of us and carry us away."

"Not necessarily," I said. "Come with me."

I believe they followed me out of curiosity. Mnqoba stayed by my side without question, but Zakhele and the warriors trudged along a few paces behind with murmurs of apprehension over the "crazy white man." I led them back through the gate in the outer wall of the kraal and around, following the wall of logs and thorn branches. The grass and dirt had been trod with a mixture of hooves and bare feet, so there was no hope in finding any particular spoor. At the kraal of Izoqa I happened upon the rear door by accident, seeing the earth beaten down by many excursions into the kraal at night over weeks. Here, I suspected there had only been a couple visitations. I ran my hand along the wall, finger tips pressing the logs as I passed along. Then one gave under my touch.

I stopped, found an opened for my fingers, and pulled four logs away as I had at the neighboring kraal. As before, these logs had been sawn at the base, wedged in together to appear solid, yet providing easy access.

I stepped through the opening, followed by the captain and the others, who looked around in astonishment.

"That is Umgibeli's hut," the captain said, pointing to the thatched dome in front of us. And that of his first wife, who was taken, as well as Liyana and one sister. There is the hut of his second wife, and the other daughters, all taken."

"You see," I said, "this isn't the work of spirits. This was done by men."

"What men?" the captain asked.

I searched the dirt around the huts but found no footprints leading to the opening in the wall. There were scratches, as though branches had been dragged across the ground. Whoever had stolen into the kraal, killed the chief, and captured his family, they went out of their way to disguise their presence, assured that their activities would be blamed on the supernatural. I was certain of only one thing. They would be back.

"There has been fighting among tribes," the captain said. "Since you English have taken away Cetewayo, the Zulu have no unity. Tribe fights tribe. We have been on good terms with the people of Izoqa, but there are others who would steal our cattle and women. They live further away, but they have troubled us before. We will gather our warriors and begin a march upon their kraal. We shall wage war and avenge Umgibeli."

The other warriors raised their assegais and cheered.

"Wait!" I said, and they stared at me as though I might be in league with the rival tribe.

"Let Macumazahn speak," Zakhele said.

The captain cocked his head to one side and waited.

"You don't know who did this," I said. "You have no idea where Liyana, her sisters, and the others were taken." I dared not say that they might already be dead, although I did not believe in that, since why carry them off if just to kill them. It would be much easier to kill any of them in the same manner as they had with Umgibeli. "Are you at least convinced that this was not done supernaturally?"

The warriors looked at one another, eventually all nodding, although their eyes told me that none of them ruled out the possibility of at least some assistance with the supernatural.

"This is exactly what happened to Izoqa's kraal," I said. "First the chief was killed, then the doctor. I believe that was done to frighten and disorient the tribe, who would blame spirits. As you have done. Then, a few at a time, people vanished. I suspect they were carried off during the night, through the opening in the kraal wall. Without any evidence of kidnapping, it would seem to be supernatural. But you have evidence in that wall. We don't know who did this, where they came from, or where they are going, but one thing is certain if matters progress as they had done with Izoqa's people. They will return."

The captain nodded thoughtfully. "And we shall be waiting for them."

"And kill them!" one man declared, stabbing his spear into the earth as emphasis, impaling an imaginary foe. Others mumbled agreement.

"No," I said.

The captain eyed me with anger at my impertinence to even suggest a different strategy, as though I usurped his command.

"They must be captured," I said. "That is the only hope Liyana and the other captives have. Maybe some of Izoqa's people are still alive. There's a good chance Umgibeli's family is, but if we kill the captors we may never find out where they were taken."

The captain nodded. "Macumazahn speaks wisdom. Let us set a trap for our crafty spirits."

CHAPTER EIGHT

Dumisani, captain to the warriors, sought out my counsel in private. He was a soldier and was used to straight-forward fighting. He had fought in some skirmishes, but primarily defended the kraal form invasion from other tribes. In his youth he had been in a regiment under Cetewayo. These days, now that Zululand was under British control, there was no war but many disagreements. Tribes fought among themselves for territory. Umgibeli had not been an ambitious chief. His people had enough land, since the kraals were far enough away from each other to not encroach on one another's grazing grounds. Dumisani's primary concerns were defensive. Now he had to learn to set a trap for an unknown enemy.

Under my suggestions, the logs in the back opening were replaced and the ground on either side of the wall swept with branches to clear away our footprints. Next, the two huts closest to the hidden opening were altered. Mud walls were cut away, supports made to keep the thatch roof from caving in, and false walls were constructed. These were woven branches covered with mud and left to dry in the sun. When they were stiff, they were set into the holes in the hut walls, blending with the actual wall. It was a shoddy job that would fool no one in broad daylight, but at night no one could tell the difference between the real wall and the false ones.

The villagers were encouraged to continue their daily chores as though nothing had changed. The cattle were driven out onto the veldt to graze during the day, and then brought into the central kraal at night. They cooked and ate meals, then retired to their huts for the evening. All during the day, herdsmen kept a surreptitious watch for strangers who might be spying from some distance. Although Mnqoba had found the remains of a cigarette that indicated a white man, we could not be certain who was responsible for the murders and kidnappings. Slave traders were mentioned, but it had been a long time since that had been a danger in Zululand. It was possible that traders had come from Transvaal or regions north to conduct the business of abductions, carry their victims over the border, and sell them either in Transvaal or more northern regions. However, abducting a few at a time made no sense. Slave traders would normally make a single raid, and then quickly move over the border to avoid capture.

As evening fell, warriors carried their assegais into the huts at the rear of the kraal. Mnqoba, Dumisani, and I entered one with the false wall. Six other warriors joined us. Ten other warriors occupied the hut opposite us. Other warriors hid in nearby huts, ready to rush out should an alarm be raised.

Mnqoba and I had rifles, and I carried my pistol. All the warriors carried short assegais and kerries.

And so we waited. And waited.

Hours passed and I found myself dozing, my head bobbing, which did not do well for my native name, Watcher-by-Night. Thankfully it was pitch dark in the hut. It was embarrassing enough without having been noticed. I would have never heard the end of it from Mnqoba.

A noise finally came. Very slight. Wood brushing against wood. The logs in the wall were being removed. The others around me stiffened, all aware of the sound. The moment had come.

Peering through a slit in our false wall, I could see the opening appear in the kraal's outer wall. Out of the darkness, an even darker shape appeared.

I could see no details, just blackness blending with the night. It moved as a man, crossing through the opening into the kraal. It was hunched, stepping silently. From inside the hut, I could not hear its footfalls.

There was something unusual about its movements. They were very slow and deliberate, but as a man who either had injuries or deformities. He was of small stature; even smaller than I. Wiry in shape. One hand clutched a stick about a foot in length and about an inch thick. This did not appear to be much of a weapon. If the intruder planned on incapacitating his victims with it, I doubt he would succeed. It was not pointed for stabbing and would break if used to whack someone over the head. Since he had no other weapons visible, I supposed he was only a scout for a larger party waiting outside.

Another curious thing I noticed as the shadowy figure approached the huts. He seemed to be naked. I could detect no clothing. He was either a black man or a white man with his skin painted or dyed black in order to move unnoticed at night.

The others on either side of me shifted nervously, as though ready to burst through and capture the intruder. I knew that there were others awaiting him outside and that if we fell upon this one scout, the others would flee. I whispered a single Zulu word for them to be still.

The figure outside instantly stopped and cocked his head. It was not possible for him to have heard me. He was not yet near our hiding place and I had spoken in such a low whisper that those at my back probably could not have heard. Perhaps someone in the other hut had stirred, as anxious as my companions had become.

After several minutes of posing as a statue, he began his cautious movements again.

He stole past the opposite hut, in order to go around the chief's hut that sat slightly forward of the cluster. Suddenly, he turned and bolted back toward the wall.

The false wall of the other hut burst outward, spilling warriors onto the path.

The shadow raised the stick he carried, putting one end to his lips.

And the first of Umgibeli's men collapsed.

Surprise no longer an issue, Mnqoba and I pushed down our own façade and rushed into the space between the huts.

He was too swift, with completely inhuman speed. Already past us, he would disappear through the opening within seconds. Yet, he took the time to stop and turn, raising up the stick once more. Mnqoba was running past me, being faster than my old limp. He crashed to the ground, rolled, and lay still.

Then the shadow tossed something at us.

There was a sudden, blinding flash, and the whole area around us was filled with thick white smoke. Between the smoke and the spots that burned my stunned eyes, I could see nothing. The Zulu around me were cursing and stumbling, bumping into each other. I tripped over Mnqoba, losing my rifle. On hands and knees in the dirt, I squeezed my eyes shut and tried to push away the spots that blinded my vision.

As the smoke began to drift away on the breeze, Dumisani called his men together to pursue the intruder. A torch was brought by the other warriors who had been waiting in other huts. In the flickering light, they formed ranks and headed toward the opening in the outer wall.

"No!" I said, blocking their way. "It's too late. They're gone."

"Then we will hunt them down," Dumisani said. "This devil killed Umgibeli. He has just now killed your friend, Mnqoba."

I bent down to examine Mnqoba and found him sound asleep.

"He's just unconscious," I said.

"What magic does this devil have that it can make sleep come from a stick?" Dumisani asked.

"No magic," I said. I lifted up a narrow sliver of wood notched with feathers, like a tiny arrow. "This was in Mnqoba's chest. I imagine what the intruder carried was not just a stick, but was hollow and used as a blowgun. He shot your man and Mnqoba with these darts."

One big warrior snatched the dart from my fingers.

"How can this tiny thing bring down a warrior?"

"I'd be careful with that," I said. "There's still a gummy residue on the tip. It could still be potent…"

My warning came too late. The warrior inadvertently punctured his finger on the pointed end of the dart. His eyes rolled back and he collapsed to the ground, unconscious.

"We must hunt the devil down," Dumisani insisted.

"Yes, but not right now," I said sternly. "If you go out there, you will ruin any spoor left behind. Our intruder left in too much of a hurry. Usually they cover up their track, but they didn't have the time for that tonight. He wasn't alone, and we have no way of telling how many were with him until we can look for footprints. And once we find those, we can track them down. Maybe even find where they've taken the captives. But we can't do that until sunrise."

"Very well, Macumazahn," Dumisani said. "Your wisdom is greater than ours in dealing with devils."

"It was no devil," I said.

"That I cannot agree with. In the moment it made that light that blinded, before the smoke, I saw its face. It looked like a man, but the face was not that of a man. Nor of the big cat. Although it was cat-like. Its nose and mouth blended like that of an animal's snout. Its ears were small and high and pointed. And its skin was covered in short black fur. It was not the panther devil that hunted our cattle, but it was no man, either."

"I would say, Dumisani, that what you saw was a trick. A disguise used to make you or anyone who happened to see the intruder to believe that it was supernatural, to frighten you into thinking it was a devil. But I know the warriors of Umgibeli are made of sterner stuff and not frightened so easily. If you were given a chance, you would see through this disguise and find only a man."

Dumisani stood straighter in pride. "As Macumazahn says. We shall tend to these who sleep, then you will lead us when the sun rises, and we will hunt down this man who thinks he can frighten a Zulu."

He left men to guard the opening, with instructions that they should not go outside and thereby disturb any tracks left behind. Mnqoba and the two unconscious warriors were carried off.

I contemplated my words to Dumisani. Was I trying to convince myself? In that moment of the flash, for that fraction of a second, the image became seared into my memory. I had seen exactly what Dumisani had seen, a man who appeared part panther. I had seen up close the panther that had killed Kennedy. There were superficial similarities, but they were two different creatures. Some amalgam of man and beast to varying degrees. I could not see how it could be a disguise, a hoax, especially in the light of the creature that originally brought us here. Was there some connection between the two? Surely it could not be coincidental that two such beasts would be in the same area. Had there been more such creatures outside the kraal, waiting for their scout? Were they responsible for the deaths and kidnappings?

I paced the confines of the kraal, nibbled dried meat, and checked on Mnqoba every few minutes, waiting impatiently for the sun to rise over the veldt.

CHAPTER NINE

The tracks we studied at sunrise were the most unusual I had ever seen. The intruder walked upon the balls of his bare feet, never leaving the indentation of his heels. The front part of the foot was longer than usual for that of a man, and thicker, as though padded. The toes were uniformly short and stubby. The prints were also wide apart, as he was running at a fantastic speed over the grassland. I had to circle obstacles as I followed them, where the creature had merely leaped over them, be they brush or log or boulder.

After a mile, I grew suspicious.

Our visitor traveled south west in almost a straight line. However, he did not cross the spoor he would have left upon his approach.

"We're being led on a wild goose chase," I said.

Dumisani scanned the grassland. "I see no geese, Macumazahn."

"No," I said. "And you won't see any tracks of his accomplices, either. He's leading us away from them so that they can get away. He's fast. We probably wouldn't have caught up with him if we had set out immediately. I'm not even certain if we could have caught him if we were on horseback. But his comrades are probably slower and needed time to get away."

"What shall we do?" Dumisani asked. "Follow these until they turn back?"

He was accompanied by twenty other warriors. Mnqoba had still not revived from the sleeping dart, so we had left him behind. I was inclined to leave some men following this spoor but thought it was a waste of time.

"We'll return and try to find the spoor of his arrival. He had no chance to cover it up, so we should find something. My mistake was following the fresher trail, thinking it would lead us to where the others were. He was more clever than I gave him credit."

Returning to the kraal, we found the original tracks easily enough. These we backtracked around the kraal and over the grass. By this time, Mnqoba was up and about and complaining of a terrible headache. He joined us as we climbed the hills overlooking the kraal.

Here, we found the spoor of our intruder's accomplices.

"White men," Dumisani said with disgust, as though he already knew who the culprits were. He pointed to the crushed grass and the occasional boot print and looked at me without any indication that I was part of the same race that he was blaming.

Mnqoba picked something off the ground and held it up between thumb and forefinger to show us. It was the stomped remains of a cigarette similar to one he had found on our previous search over the hills for signs of the other panther creature.

"Definitely white men," he said.

We followed their tracks, which led to the spoor of horses that had been held in wait, and from there the spoor came from the northwest and returned in that direction. Eventually they were obscured by other tracks of small antelope herds.

As it grew late, we returned to the kraal before dark.

"There is only one white settlement in that direction," Dumisani said at the evening meal, where he paced in front of the cooking fire. "The Boer kraal. Those white men must be from the Boer kraal."

"Umgibeli said that the Boers were killed when his father was chief," I said.

"Then they are from another kraal," Dumisani said, "or they have returned to the one that lay empty. We will hunt these white devils down and kill them."

"Let's just make certain we have the right culprits," I said. "We don't want British troops marching in here and punishing you. In fact, we can ride to the nearest outpost or send a runner, and have the government look into the affair."

"By that time," Mnqoba said, "Liyana would be lost. And the others," he added quickly.

"We must attack now!" Dumisani said.

Others grumbled in agreement.

"If they are abducting people from the kraals," I said, "they must be involved in the slave trade. It has not been active around here in many years, but with Transvaal's independence, some enterprising men may have started it up again or decided to expand on their territory or they are merely passing through Transvaal from other areas. I can't see a single Boer farm being implicated in abducting so many slaves. They couldn't possibly keep such an activity secret. They would eventually bring the colonial government down on them."

Although evidence pointed toward the Boer settlement, as it was the closest where white men lived, or had lived, and was in the right direction, I did not want to encourage an all out attack. The settlement might still be abandoned, or some totally innocent people may have moved in after the original owners had been killed. The murderers and kidnappers may be from somewhere else. If these warriors had their way, there might be another Battle of Isandlwana, with fewer players on hand. With tensions as they were after recent events, with Cetewayo in exile in England, Zululand under the British, and various tribes fighting for dominance, the slaughter of a settlement of whites could trigger another war. I often found myself on the edge of great historical events, and I did not want this to grow into one.

"I'll go to this Boer kraal and investigate it," I said. "If I see any sign of your missing people, I'll return and we'll discuss how best to return them, or avenge them."

Dumisani was not pleased. He looked at me closely, as though seeing me for the first time and realizing I was white. "Macumazahn, you have a reputation for being a friend to the Zulu people, but this is not your fight. There has been talk that you have returned to the great land of your Queen and made that your home, that you have left Africa as a rich man. This is a matter for the Zulu."

"I am no different than I was before," I said, "when I stood before your kings. I want these people who killed your chiefs and stole your people to be punished, but I do not want to see another war between the Zulu and the British. If you go to the white men's kraal in your anger, you may kill them without evidence. Let me find that evidence first, so that you do not punish innocent lives and allow the evil doers to escape."

Dumisani thought for a time. His brow furrowed and his eyes reflected an inner conflict. He was a soldier, used to following commands, passing them down to the warriors under him. He was also a herdsman, tending cattle as often as he trained his men to fight. They were no longer at war, although they lived under the threat of other tribes and other chiefs trying to fill the void left by Cetewayo's absence. With his chief gone, Dumisani was thrust into a position he was not prepared for. He was responsible for the entire tribe. If he was taking my words to heart, he was also weighing the consequences that could affect the whole of the Zulu people.

He stood up, some of his anger gone, but his face still wrestling with emotions. "I will think upon this. I will let you know my decision at sunrise."

With that he walked away, although he did not retire to his hut.

As I headed for my wagon for the night, Mnqoba followed me. An antithesis to Dumisani's somberness, he was nervous, anxiety making him move and talk quickly.

"Macumazahn, we must go now. We cannot delay. We must follow the white men's trail. We must save Liyana and the others."

"Can we follow spoor on a moonless night?" I asked. "Get some rest, for we will start at daybreak, regardless of Dumisani's decision. If he chooses to run off half cocked, then we will go with him. Perhaps there will be some way for us to avoid a massacre. If he allows us to go ahead and act as scouts to investigate the settlement, then we must start early. Either way, we will be travelling."

In the morning, after a quick breakfast, Mnqoba and I yoked the oxen team and prepared to leave.

Dumisani approached me and I could see by the hollowness around his eyes that he had not slept.

"Macumazahn, if it had not been for you, we would not have known what befell our chief and our people. You have shown us how the intruder came in to commit murder and kidnapping. You have shown that the panther man is in league with white men. We do not blame all white men. We want only those guilty to be punished. To bring vengeance on innocent people would make us worse than those who have hurt us. I grant you some days to see if the old Boer kraal is inhabited and whether who might be there are guilty or innocent. Zakhele will travel with you, as he is familiar with the way. While you are gone, I will send runners to other kraals to see if any other tribes have been afflicted by these crimes. I will also try to gather forces with other tribes that we may come against the guilty white men in force and be prepared for the consequences from the British. If we do not hear word from you in five days, we will attack the Boer kraal. Is that reasonable to you, Watcher-by-Night?"

As he talked, a glum looking Zakhele approached with his assegai and a skin bag slung over one shoulder carrying supplies.

"It's reasonable," I told Dumisani. "If you fight, do it with a level head and not out of anger."

He turned away, calling for runners to send his messages.

I climbed onto the wagon box and drove the team forward, Mnqoba and Zakhele guiding the oxen through the gate of the kraal. We began our long journey northwest, while I was filled with apprehension over what we would find. More than likely, the place would be abandoned since the original settlers were killed, overgrown and in ruin. Other Boers may have moved in, but this was southeast of Transvaal. Boers would likely stay within the borders of Transvaal and out of Zululand.

I did not expect to find evidence of the missing tribe members. They had probably been carried further into the interior, or to areas unfriendly to England, to be sold into slavery. The Boers of Transvaal may have returned to trading in slavery, in which case colonial authorities needed to be informed. Especially if they were raiding areas under British protection. The captives might even be carried off to other territories. To take people a few at a time, to eventually empty a whole village, rather than bring in an armed force and take everyone at once, was an unusual tactic. I wondered who might be behind this travesty, and how these panther men fit into the equation. Could the slavers have found some lost, isolated race of beast men and were forcing them to help in their illicit trade?

Two days of travel brought us to a grassy area that funneled into a kloof. On the right of the gorge sat a large house that overlooked the veldt. Behind it, kraals for cattle and outbuildings were visible. Cattle dotted the hills, while goats grazed in a pen behind the house. Further into the shadows of the kloof, behind the house, stood a barn that had seen better days but still seemed solid. Near it was another outbuilding, long and low like a bunk house. The main house itself was wide, single story, with a long veranda in front. It appeared well-kept and far from abandoned. Flowers bloomed on either side of the stone steps leading up to the veranda.

As our team drew near, a middle-aged man in white linen and cradling a double barreled shotgun appeared out the front door.

"I say," I called out, "could you help us? We seem a bit lost."

"Who are you?" the man asked as he descended the steps, never raising the shotgun in any threatening manner, but not losing the suspicion that shaded his eyes.

"Name's Quatermain. I was doing a bit of hunting and got turned around."

I climbed down from the wagon and approached him, reaching out my hand. He shifted his weapon so that he could return the gesture, and we shook.

"Blake. Emerson Blake." He was an Englishman about my own age, middle to late fifties, with thinning gray hair and a tall, thin build. A pair of spectacles perched on his nose. His suspicion evaporated at my disarming approach, though he made annoyed glances at Mnqoba and Zakhele.

"I didn't expect to meet anyone this far out, especially an Englishman," I said. "My man said this used to be a Boer settlement."

"Oh, yes. Used to be. I bought it just over two years ago, had it rebuilt. But where are my manners? Please, come into the shade for refreshment. Your men can take your oxen to a kraal behind the house and water them."

I nodded to Mnqoba to take the wagon behind the house, giving him

"Could you help us? We seem a bit lost."

a quick look that meant for him and Zakhele to have a surreptitious look around, while I followed our host to the veranda.

"Kuan-yin!" he called out. "We have guests."

At his beckoning, a small Chinese man appeared at the door in the white outfit of a house servant and bowed low.

"Yes, Doctor Blake."

"Some tea, Kuan-yin. With some of that cake. And our guest has two men seeing to their ox team out back. See that they have some fresh water and something to eat."

"Yes, Doctor Blake."

The servant disappeared into the dark interior of the house and Blake motioned me to a pair of wicker chairs. I took off my hat and sat down.

"Thank you for your hospitality, Doctor. Are you a medical practitioner?" I asked.

"Retired," he said wearily as he sank upon the other chair. "I grew tired of my London practice and came out here for a change."

"This isn't normally a place where one comes for a quiet retirement," I said. "The English countryside is more in keeping with the tradition." I thought of the Grange, my own place in Yorkshire, so recently purchased at Sir Henry's insistence.

Blake laughed. "Ah, well, I have always had an interest in the Dark Continent. I practically devoured everything Burton wrote and I've followed Stanley quite closely. And I met Francis Galton and sat in many of his lectures, some dealing with his time in Africa. But my medical career took precedence. My father would have none of me running off and exploring the world. Now I have gained enough money through my career and an inheritance that I could finally come here and make a homestead."

"My son Harry is presently in medical school in London," I said.

"What a coincidence. Tell me, what school?" he asked, brightening.

Kuan-yin returned with a silver tray laden with a tea set and china plates with cakes. He set the tray on a wicker table between the two chairs and proceeded to pour the tea into cups, handing one to Blake, and then one to me. Without a word, he bowed to Blake and slipped back into the house. We chatted for a time, as we ate cake and drank cups of Darjeeling. My impression of Blake was that of an educated gentleman. He was open and friendly, and I felt no guile in him whatsoever. He appeared to be exactly what he claimed to be. I found no inconsistencies in his story or his general conversation. There was absolutely no evidence that he was behind any type of slave trade.

It was with a sense of relief that I allowed myself to be engrossed in our conversation, which I kept away from myself and guided toward his own history. I allowed him to believe that my home was in England, as it now was, and that I was merely visiting Natal for a hunting expedition, which had been my original intent, with the late Kennedy. Details I skirted, although I felt guilty over lying through omission. I became convinced that Blake had nothing to do with either the murders and abductions or the mysterious panther men.

I became even more certain when the door opened and a young woman came onto the veranda.

She appeared to be in her middle thirties, with a pleasant oval face, blond hair wrapped in a loose bun, and startling blue eyes. She smiled as she saw me, exposing white teeth with one askew on the side, which did not distract from her attractiveness but seemed to add to it.

I stood immediately, setting aside my tea cup and saucer.

She reached out her hand and I took it.

"Hello. Kuan-yin said we had visitors. I'm Emma."

"Allan," I said. "Allan Quatermain. It's a pleasure to meet you, Mrs. Blake."

She laughed heartily, giving Blake an amused glance, which he did not seem to appreciate. "No. We aren't married. And before your think me improper, we are not attached in any romantic way, either. Emerson was partners with my late husband, James. We moved here together two years ago, and James passed away a short time later. The house and property are half mine and I've nowhere else to go, so here I stay. An unusual arrangement, but, as you see, we are very far away from the prying eyes of modern sensibilities that would condemn what they see and not what they know. Emerson and my husband were friends and partners for many years, and I assisted them in their endeavors. We remain friends."

"I am very sorry for the loss of your husband," I said, recalling the bitterness of my own losses so many years ago.

She looked at me thoughtfully for a time, as though measuring my earnestness. "Thank you," she eventually said.

"If you don't mind," she said, "I'll leave you gentlemen talk. I'll see Jiaying about dinner. It's getting late. You'll stay the night, I hope, Mr. Quatermain. We have plenty of room."

"I don't want to impose," I said.

"Nonsense. Jiaying is an excellent cook. And we have a spare room that has never been used. We never get any guests. It's a pleasure to have new company. No offence, Emerson."

"Thank you, Mrs. Er…"

"Just Emma, Mr. Quatermain."

"Allan," I said.

She smiled her little crooked smile, her blue eyes shining. "Allan."

I watched as she entered the house, then noticed Blake's expression. Before I looked at him, he allowed a darkness to pass over his face, as though a bit of jealousy clouded it. In a moment it was gone, but I suspected that his feelings for the widow were something more than just friendship, as she had insisted. Perhaps she was not aware of them or perhaps Blake refrained from expressing them since she had been so recently widowed.

"A terrible tragedy that she should lose her husband so soon after moving here," I said.

"Yes," he agreed. "Terrible. Add to that the loss of their son only months before."

I looked at him in shock, thinking that the death of a child must be the worst experience. I have lost parents, spouses, and dear friends over my long years, but if I ever lost Harry … "How awful! How old was he?"

"Twenty."

I had to re-evaluate my estimation as to the young lady's age.

"The one reason she agreed with her husband and me to emigrate here was because of her son. He was the only relative she had, other than James. Her son was a corporal with the 2nd Warwickshire Regiment. He was killed at Isandlwana two years ago."

The infamous battle that led to the downfall of Cetewayo and the Zulu Empire.

I nodded understanding, not knowing what to say, refraining to add that I had been there. I had witnessed the devastation of that battle, had been in the thick of things, yet had survived when so many others had not. Since I had led Blake to believe my home was in England, I did not want to complicate matters by admitting my involvement in the Battle of Isandlwana. Questions would arise that I did not want to answer, and perhaps resentment that I survived when Emma's son had not. I wondered how the husband met his end, for sometimes grief does terrible things; but I would not pry and Blake did not volunteer.

"Poor thing," Blake went on, looking at the front door of the house. "She has no one now. No family to go back to England for. Nothing there, not even the home they knew. It was sold before we left. Nothing but memories. She has enough money to return and start a new life, but she no longer has the desire. She insists she won't leave her son and husband, whose graves are on that hill overlooking the house."

He pointed to the right, and under the shade of a mimosa on the hilltop I could make out two wooden crosses marking the final resting places of her son and husband.

As the sun grew closer to the horizon, a man on horseback came riding toward the house, driving a herd of about twenty cattle ahead of him. Behind the herd rode two other men.

"Ah, that's Josef," Blake said. "Our cattleman. We hired him early on, since he's from the area and knows his cattle. Used to have a herd of his own, and a homestead, until the Zulu uprising. They took his cattle, but fortunately spared his life."

As he passed the house, Josef gave me a nod of greeting, then immediately shouted curses in Dutch at his men who were having trouble with stragglers.

Emma opened the front door and poked her head out. "Dinner will be ready soon, Allan. Perhaps you would like an opportunity to freshen up."

"Thank you, yes," I said, standing.

Blake stood also. "Go inside. I'll talk to Josef and have him see to your boys."

I followed Emma into the wide entranceway, and she directed me to their spare room, which she explained would be mine for the evening. A bowl and pitcher of fresh water was available, along with clean towels.

"If you need anything," she said, "just ask Kuan-yin. He'll wait outside to show you to the dining room."

"Are all your servants Chinese?" I asked.

"Yes."

"No one local? Even to help with the cattle?"

"Josef is in charge of the herd," she said. "He has some other Boers who work under him. I suppose Boers could be considered local. But if you mean natives, no."

With that she walked out, leaving me with her last words sounding bitter. Understandable, I thought at the time. Her son was killed by Zulu. She may have seen any local native as Zulu and attributed bad feelings toward them, blaming them for her son's death. As I mentioned, grief can do terrible things.

Kuan-yin led me to the dining room, where Emma sat at one end and Blake at the other. The room was paneled and furnished with a fine oak table with six chairs, looking like any from a number of manors from the English countryside. The china was some of the finest I had seen, putting to shame my own dishware at the Grange.

A petite young Chinese woman named Jiaying, who was also the cook, served the meal of rice and vegetables, with bits of chicken in a sweet sauce. Emma called the dish by a Chinese name, which, she explained, were the only dishes Jiaying could accomplish. She scorned Western cuisine, which was fine with her and Blake, although Blake made a distasteful expression for a brief moment, leading me to believe that he missed plain meals.

The door opened, and into the dining room strode Josef, his hands and face cleaned of dust and his clothes fresh.

"You must be Quatermain," he said, reaching out a big, callused hand toward me.

"*Goeienaand*," I said, quite out of instinct.

He grinned. "Ah, you speak Dutch. Good. We can have a chat and my employers will have no idea what I am saying about them."

Blake laughed. "Tell him all our secrets, Josef."

"Oh, my goodness, no!" Emma said in mocking shock, placing one palm over her mouth. "And ruin our reputation?"

"Your reputation is safe with me," I assured her.

She looked at me closely and said, just under her breath so that only I heard, "A pity."

The dinner was fine and the conversation light. I was asked what my vocation was, and I replied that I was a retired trader, living off the earnings of a lucrative investment. I did not mention the investment had been gems from King Solomon's mines, or that I had traded furs and ivory across South Africa in my younger days. As the last plates were taken away, Josef bid everyone good night and left through the back of the house. Blake yawned and said that he was ready to retire for the evening.

"Mind if I have a smoke on the veranda before turning in?" I asked my hosts, pulling my pipe from my pocket. "It's a habit of mine after a good meal and before sleeping."

"Not at all, old fellow," Blake said. "Just don't go wandering around. Lions, you know. The house lights keep them away, but they like to stray close because of the goats and cattle. Josef usually has one of his Boers on guard during the night, but you never know where the buggers will turn up."

I also knew that there were no lions in the area, but didn't mention it.

I slipped onto the veranda, stuffed my pipe, and struck a match to it. Standing on the edge of the steps, I looked out over the rolling grassland bathed in starlight. It was a wonderfully peaceful scene, and I was tempted to stretch out in one of the wicker chairs, smoke, and doze. But my intention was to stroll around the house and to the rear, in order to speak with Mnqoba and Zakhele, who surely had time to look around. They would probably be sleeping in the wagon.

No doubt there was nothing to be discovered and we could return to Umgibeli's kraal and make our report, so that Dumisani would not bring the warriors of half a dozen tribes down upon Blake and Emma, thereby killing innocent people and incurring the wrath of the colonial government. Once that tragedy was avoided, we could report to that very same government of the abductions and probable slave trading occurring on colonial soil. I did not like being the catalyst to another conflict between the colonies and the Boers, but I could not tolerate slavery.

As I stepped off the veranda I heard the door behind me open and someone step out. I figured it was Blake about to warn me about nonexistent lions.

The fragrance of the flowers on either side of the stone steps wafted over me, pushing away the smell of tobacco.

"It is beautiful, isn't it," Emma said as she approached the steps.

I turned to her and realized that the floral scent had come from her and not the bedded flowers. She looked out over the starlit veldt.

"Yes," I said, and tore my eyes from her to glance once more at the scenery.

"I miss England," she said, "but I would surely miss this more if I were ever to leave. Except for the bugs. I should never miss the bugs."

We both laughed and she joined me at the bottom of the step. She wrapped her arm around mine and we walked away from the house, Emma staring up at the sky.

"In England," she said, "I never realized there were so many stars. Look at them, Allan. It's amazing."

I should have been uncomfortable from her closeness, for we had just met and she had gone through such tragedies so recently. Yet it felt natural. Not that I had any romantic inclinations. I was much older than she. In the morning I would be gone from her home and on my way back to England in a few weeks, and she would forget all about my visit.

"You said you were on a hunting expedition," she said eventually. "How long had you planned to travel?"

"A few weeks," I said. "And then back to England with some trophies."

The pang of guilt turned the meal in my stomach. I did not like lying to her. Certain things were true, but I was misleading her. Shouldn't I be telling her the truth, that we were on the trail of slavers and that she and Blake should take precautions? If the slavers came through their territory they may just as easily kill her and Blake and everyone here in order to keep their secret.

We walked around the house, past the kraal of dozing cattle and my own oxen, who were separated by fencing. My wagon sat near by, and I heard someone stirring inside. The canvas flap at the rear parted slightly.

Heavy boots sounded on the hard earth, and a man carrying a rifle came from the far end of the kraal, where a barn and the other building stood. I took the second structure to be the living quarters for the hands.

"*Goedenavond, Mevrouw* Cairns," the man said in a thick Dutch accent.

"Good evening, Pieter." As we passed the kraals and walked to the other side of the house, Emma patted my arm. "Pieter is on first watch tonight. There is always a danger of predators, and the native population is not always friendly."

"How many men do you have?" I asked.

"Oh, a few. But we can always use one more," she added, leaving me still wondering if there were enough armed men to defend the homestead against a band of wandering slavers. "Are you volunteering, Allan?"

I felt my face flush and was grateful for the darkness.

"No," I said. "But I'd like to make certain you have enough men to keep you safe."

"That's very kind of you. It's a pleasure to have you here, Allan. Someone intelligent and compassionate to talk with. Josef and his men, they can be a bit lacking when it comes to intelligent conversation."

"Surely Blake …"

"Oh, Emerson is brilliant. He and my husband were the smartest people I have ever known. But sometimes being so intelligent there are sacrifices to other aspects of personality, such as compassion. Emerson can be cold and calculating and impersonal."

"If I am not being impertinent, he doesn't look at you in an impersonal manner."

"Oh, we are just friends. Perhaps he wishes for more, but that will never happen. Poor Emerson is two dimensional. His career was everything to him, so much so that he lacks imagination. His interests are narrow. Sometimes I would just like to talk about mundane things, like the weather in the English countryside, what new shows are playing in London, what are the fashions in Paris, what new book has caught the fancy of the public."

"As to the theater," I said, "I must claim ignorance. My friend, Sir

Henry, had introduced me to some play and I admit that I dozed off part way through. And as for fashion of any kind, I know even less. I do occasionally read modern literature. An American, who has recently passed away, presented me with a copy of a new novel that is very popular in his country, *Ben-Hur*. I read it on the voyage to the Cape. I believe it is with my belongings in my wagon, in case you would be interested in reading it. It was quite good."

"Thank you. I seldom receive anything new to read, even newspapers. I do get tired of all the medical and scientific journals that fill our meager library."

We chatted of other things, and when we once again reached the steps to the veranda, Emma stifled a yawn. "I'm afraid I must turn in."

"And I will follow as soon as I clean out my pipe," I said.

"Goodnight, Allan. If you must leave tomorrow, I do hope you will come our way again."

"I shall do my best," I said. "Goodnight."

As the door closed, I cursed myself for my deception. The poor woman had been through so much, and here I was lying to her. Even when she was retiring for the night, I had lied. I did clean out my pipe and pocket it, but my intention was to skulk back to my wagon. I argued that I was essentially protecting her. Obviously she and Blake were not involved with the abductions from the local kraals. Emma was not capable of that, let alone murdering the chieftains and witch doctors. The only darkness I gathered from Blake had been his jealousy where Emma was concerned. He obviously cared for the widow and refused to intervene on her mourning, yet saw me as a potential threat to any imagined intimacy. He would be doomed to disappointment for, although I would not seek any romantic entanglement, Emma was not interested in Blake in that way.

I slipped back the way we had come, circling the house. I could hear the heavy footsteps of Pieter as he patrolled the kraal and could tell that he was on the other side of the house, heading to the front. The cattle stirred slightly and a goat bleated as I covered the distance to the wagon parked next to the wood plank fencing.

Mnqoba gave a startled cry as I pulled aside the canvas flap over the rear of the wagon.

"Be quiet you fool!" I snapped.

"Sorry, Macumazahn. I did not expect you. I saw you with the lady."

Toward the front of the wagon, Zakhele stirred, then began snoring.

"Were you able to learn anything?" I asked.

"Very little, Macumazahn. There are Boers here working the cattle. I saw three of them. One brought us food and water, but they have kept an eye on us, always one of them watching us. I do not think they like us."

"That's understandable, since Umgibeli's tribe had killed the Boers who originally settled here."

"Considering their attitude toward us, there might have been reason for that. Slavery is often a good reason to kill the slavers."

"Not all Boers condone slavery, let alone are involved in the trade," I said.

"No, but it only takes one man to be a slaver to destroy many lives," Mnqoba said.

"I don't believe these people are involved in abduction and slavery. I've talked with the owners, a man named Blake and the woman you saw me with. She's a widow and he was her husband's friend, a doctor from England. Two of the most unlikely people to be involved with slavers. More than likely they are in danger of the real slavers coming through here and killing them as witnesses to the crime. At the very least, they are in danger of Dumisani leading a raid on them. We need to get back to Umgibeli's kraal and tell Dumisani these people are innocent."

"What about their Boer workers?" Mnqoba asked. "I do not trust them."

"How could a couple of workers be able to sneak away, kidnap all those people, and sell them all into slavery without their bosses knowing? You said yourself there are only three."

"I said I only saw three. There could be many more."

"Or no more. Don't let your imagination run wild, Mnqoba."

"Those two buildings are large for just three men."

"One's a barn. A storage building. The other is a bunkhouse of sorts, for the hands to live in. If it makes you feel any better, I'll take a look in them before I go to bed."

He made to climb out of the wagon. "I will go with you."

"No. Stay here. If they find me sneaking about, I'll just tell them I couldn't sleep. With you, it looks more suspicious. Besides, you are noisy."

"I am not! I am as silent as a leopard stalking its prey. I proved that with those two men whose boots I stole and threw into the tree."

"Just stay in the wagon and you won't get into any trouble."

I left him protesting and circled the kraal, heading for the barn, all the while listening for Pieter on his patrol. The double door to this building had a chain wrapped over the handles and a padlock. I peeked through the crack between the doors and saw the inky blackness beyond. After a moment, my eyes adjusted and I could make out the frame of a wagon, parked just inside. I could also smell leather, which attested to saddles or harnesses, at least the tack used to strap oxen to the wagon yokes. I left the barn behind and walked over to the other building. I heard voices from inside and saw lights from one window. Peering in, I saw Josef and two others at a table playing cards. In the back area of the room were bunks for several more men.

I could hear Pieter in the distance, coming close to the barn, so I put this bunk house between us and went to the far side of the building, which was in darkness. The door at this end was unlocked, and I slipped inside.

The room in which I found myself was engulfed in darkness, but I could make out items in the gloom. Cabinets lined the walls. A table in the middle had padding and hinges and reminded me of an examination table in a physician's office. Alcohol was a predominant odor. I poked through some of the cabinets, finding a variety of medical instruments, an assortment of bandages, and jars of chemicals I had no idea of their use, as the scientific names on the labels were a mystery and it was difficult to read them in the dark.

Blake and Emma's late husband had both been doctors. It was not unreasonable that they would make an unused room into a surgery office, to treat any injuries that might occur on their property. I have even known doctors to have clinics in their homes to treat locals. Although the room was unusual, it was not without precedence. I tried an inner door and found it locked. Satisfied, I returned to the outside door, listened, and stole out into the night.

I could hear Pieter's footsteps on the nearer side of the barn and closed the door as quietly as possible.

I returned to the house without incident, satisfied that nothing odd was going on here. There were no abducted people hidden away, no strange creatures, no evidence Blake, Emma, or the others were involved in any degree with the slave trade. I would be able to return to the room on loan to me and sleep a peaceful sleep, anxious to return to Dumisani in the morning and prevent a terrible tragedy.

As I stepped onto the veranda, something stung the back of my neck.

Reaching back, my fingers found a tiny wood shaft sticking out of my skin. I pulled it free and examined the shaft and the feathery end. Where had I seen something similar?

Drowsiness overcame me and I grabbed for the nearest wicker chair. If I was able to sink into it, I could take a little rest, doze for a time. I never made the chair but fell toward the plank floor. I was asleep before I landed, realizing where I had seen a similar dart.

CHAPTER TEN

My dreams were convoluted. I was in Zululand, then England. My little bungalow in Natal had rooms as large as those in the Grange in Yorkshire. One moment I was speaking to Emma Cairns, and suddenly I was conversing with Izula. I saw many people from my past, swimming in and out. Marie and Stella, my beloved wives from so long ago. Hans, loyal servant and friend since my youth, who had saved my life while sacrificing his. My father. All long gone. Even Mameena, who lurked in the shadows. Beautiful yet evil Mameena. Did this mean I was dead? No, Izula informed me. And then I was talking with Sir Henry and Captain Good.

You must awaken, Izula said. Or was it Mameena. Or perhaps Zikali.
Tell Mnqoba I am sorry.

My eyes shot open, my mind echoing with the voice of Izula.

I lay where I was, my head threatening to explode at the slightest movement. The dark room was strange, yet the mattress under me felt comfortingly familiar. All the faces that had appeared in my dreams haunted me now, and I felt as though I was coming out of a fevered sleep. My head was full of fog. I could not remember where I had been, but I was certain I had not been in bed. The odor of my own body assailed me. I must have sweated heavily. My clothes clung to me. It may have been from fever, or merely because the room was stifling. I gritted my teeth and squeezed tight my eyes, then moved. Fireworks exploded across my closed eyelids.

Easing my feet to the floor, I sat up, then dropped my aching head into my hands, fingers pushing hard against my temples.

When the room stopped swirling around me, I opened one eye.

I was not in Yorkshire. This was my house in Durban. The morning sun sent a few stray rays through the shutters, providing a little light that stung my eye. Yet it was enough to see the familiar furnishings and walls, now empty of personal belongings. No pictures on the walls, no clothes hanging in the wardrobe.

I climbed precariously to my feet, making several tries at it until finally succeeding.

Staggering to the door, I threw it open and fell through to the living room. Nothing seemed out of the ordinary. The chairs were still where they had always been. The shelves were bare and the walls empty, but then I had sent everything to England. When? Yesterday … last week. Months ago. Some crates and bundles sat piled next to the front door, with my guns leaning upon them, as though I was prepared for a trip.

Indeed, I had just been on one. A hunting trip, with tragic results.

I sank into one of the chairs, cradling my head in my hands, piecing together my recent life. The fog began to clear as I recalled Kennedy and his terrible end. Then there was the hunt for the panther creature, which eventually led to uncovering the abduction of natives by slavers. And then the old Boer settlement now inhabited by an Englishman and woman. Blake and Emma. I had been their guest, but I couldn't recall what happened.

I could not tell how much time had passed as I sat there, head in hand, battling against the ache that surged through my head, trying to push away the mist that clouded my memories. When someone knocked at my door, I started. I would have shouted for them to go away after their second knock, but my dry throat only cracked with incomprehensible gibberish.

They were persistent and patient.

Eventually, I climbed to my feet and shuffled to the door. I contemplated grabbing one of my guns that leaned against the stack of supplies and articles, but in my present condition I was just as likely to shoot my own foot than to frighten off unwanted visitors.

I swung open the door and glared at the intruder, squinting painfully against the morning sun.

"Good morning, Mr. Quatermain!"

The disgustingly cheerful face was vaguely familiar. I had seen that face recently. He wore a crisp white linen suit, unusually clean, and a white straw hat that bore no signs of extended wear. I recalled he had something to do with the colonial government.

He lost his smile as he looked at me.

"I say, old fellow, you look absolutely dreadful. When I heard you were back and in a terrible state, I didn't realize just how bad. Should I bring the doctor back?"

"Doctor?" I croaked. "What doctor?"

"You look awful," he said. "Here, let me help you sit down."

Closing the door behind him, he took my arm and led me toward the chairs. He helped me to sit down, then took the chair next to mine.

"Word came to me that you were brought back to Durban in a state of fever, that you had fallen ill on some trip into Zululand. A doctor had been called in and had given you some medication. At least you're up and around, in a way. I didn't realize how bad you must have been until I saw you just now. I had to stop by to see if there was anything I could do for you. You are, of sorts, a celebrity in these parts. We can't have anything happening to you. I'll bring the doctor around, and I'll have someone come by to help you, get you some meals. Looks like you haven't eaten for a while, but then I suppose you couldn't in your state."

I suddenly remembered the man and his visit after Kennedy's death. He had been anxious for me to catch the next boat to England.

"You're Mortimer," I said.

He beamed at me. "Yes, Mr. Quatermain. I understand that fever can play tricks on the memory. In time, everything should sort itself out."

"I'm a bit famished," I said. "I think I'll see if I have any tins in the pantry."

"Oh, no, that won't do. Not at all. I'll get someone to prepare something for you. Let me just help you back to bed, and I'll arrange everything."

He helped me to my feet, at which the room swirled around me in a whirlwind.

When I opened my eyes again, I was lying in my bed, my head propped up, the shutters and shades open to allow light and a warm breeze to flow through the house. On the breeze came the delicious aroma that reminded me of chicken soup.

A large black woman sat on a stool next to the bed. She gave me a huge smile, removed a damp cloth from my forehead, and held up a ceramic bowl with the fragrant broth.

"Ah, *inkosi*, you are awake. I have some broth for you if you are ready. I am Kaya. Do you remember me?"

I nodded, then regretted it for my head pounded as a result. "Don't you work for Dr. McKinney?"

"Yes. It is the doctor who treated you when they brought you home. The government man, Mortimer, paid me to nurse you. Here, have some broth. Then I will help you bathe."

"That's not necessary," I said, easing myself up so that I could take a spoonful of broth.

She lost her smile and became very serious, with a slightly disagreeable turn of her mouth. "Yes it is," she said. "Trust me."

"What happened to me?" I asked.

"Fever," she said.

"How did I get back to Durban?"

"Someone brought you."

"Obviously. Who? Mnqoba? Where is he?"

She shrugged. "I do not know. I only know that you had fever. You were sick for many days. Delirious. Dr. McKinney came and treated you."

"But who sent for the doctor? If it was Mnqoba, why isn't he here?"

"I do not know. Dr. McKinney does not confide in me. I did not come here until the government man asked for someone. That is all I know."

"Go and ask him. I must know what happened and where Mnqoba is."

"Yes. After I have done my job." Her tone was condescending.

I became indignant and grabbed the bowl of broth from her. "Now."

Her pleasantness evaporated and she got up. "You are still very sick, *inkosi*. You need care."

"I need answers," I said. I could remember very little from my visit to Blake's home. I recalled Emma and our conversations, but reality faded in and out. I could not recall where we talked. Was it at the dinner table, on the veranda, or on a walk around the grounds? I could not say that I was fond of her, but I felt empathy for her because of her recent losses. She was attractive, intelligent, and strong-willed. She was also in danger. Bits of memory came back, like jigsaw pieces scattered over a table. I recognized some, such as the abductions in the native kraals. And the strange man-like panthers. Slave traders were on the move. Mnqoba and I ... and Zakhele ... we had gone to Blake and Emma's home to search for signs of slavers. Dumisani ... he was seeking help from other kraals and would attack Blake's kraal because they were the nearest white people. Had Mnqoba reached Dumisani in time to stop an assault?

Kaya left in indignation.

I finished her broth and felt revived. I climbed out of bed, fought vertigo, and set about cleaning myself up. I was tremendously weak. My hunger was not sated. I needed something more substantial than broth. At least the throbbing headache was not as debilitating as it had been. I was able to get around in a way, frustrating as it was. But I was determined. I needed to find Mnqoba. I needed answers.

Relatively clean and wearing fresh clothes, I stumbled from my house into the heat of the afternoon. My legs were weak, but I gathered them under me and made a hike to the road where I could hail a rickshaw. I was carried into Durban to the nearest hotel, the Royal, where I headed for the restaurant. The maitre'd recognized me, giving me a startled look. My face was drawn, my eyes hollow. I looked as though I had just crawled from death's door, an all-to-familiar place for me. I asked for a table at the

"…where I could hail a rickshaw."

back, away from everyone, was seated, and made a quick order of steak. I had no idea if my stomach, unused to any solid food for many days, would be able to take the meal, but I was starving.

When the sizzling meal arrived, along with a cool glass of milk, I nearly swooned from the aroma. I tore into the steak with knife and fork, but forced myself to take pause before placing the first bite in my mouth. I had been in similar situations, nearly dying of thirst or starvation upon treks across desert or grassland or over mountain ranges. My inclination was to shovel food in, which would have devastating results. I took a small bite, savoring the flavor and taking time to chew. I made myself wait before taking a second bite. Then a little milk. In this manner, I dined, taking my time, in a secluded corner, away from prying eyes of the curious.

"Quatermain old chap, you look awful."

I could not escape notice from everyone. Bertram Pruet was a trader as I had been, but his shooting skills were limited so he had never gained a reputation as a hunter unless it was for being very bad. Pruet was older than I, into his sixth decade and looking every moment of it. Frizzy white hair and a white stubble covering his face, bent shoulders, and a thin frame that looked like it would be blown away in a strong wind. He was also known to cheat his customers and exaggerate his merchandise.

"Hello, Bertie, it's nice to see you, too."

He sat down across from me, uninvited, which was his way of often gaining a free meal or at least a free drink. I did not begrudge him the drink, as I called the waiter over for him to order one, but a meal was out of the question, since I did not want him around that long. I did, however, want some information, and liquor quickly loosened Bertie Pruet's tongue.

"Thought you retired, old fellow," he said as he accepted my offer of a beverage and took a large and expensive whiskey. "Struck it rich and ran off to England to live in a great mansion. Knighthood or something like that."

"Nothing like that," I said. "My son is studying in England. I wanted to be closer to him."

"Good for you. My own son won't have anything to do with me, but then his mother was the same way, after the first month of wedded bliss. Don't even know where they are. Ireland or Wales. So, are you back for good?"

"Just a short trip that didn't go well."

He looked me over. "No, I'll say it hasn't. You look all done for. Bad trip, eh? Didn't get attacked by any of the locals? Some of those fellows are still upset over our taking Zululand and a few of them are trying to take Cetewayo's place. At least things are settled with the Boers."

"Nothing like that. Do you know a man named Mnqoba?"

"Mnqoba … Mnqoba. Sounds familiar. Might have used the fellow a time or two."

"Have you seen him lately?" I asked.

"No, can't say I have. Not for months. Been away, too. Picking up some ivory from the Kalahari." Which meant that he traded for ivory which had been harvested from Kalahari elephants. He was no hunter to go after it himself.

I didn't expect much from him about Mnqoba, but it was worth a try.

When he was into his second whiskey, I asked, "Have you heard anything about slavers."

"Slavers? Ah, well, of course there's still some of that going on. Can't get rid of it all, you know, especially further into the interior. Anything specific?"

"How about anything with Transvaal?"

"Oh, those Boers were always upset about our silly old laws against slavery, but I haven't heard of any movement to bring it back. Probably a few pockets here and there, over the border. Of course, they can do whatever they want now that they're independent. None of my business, what I always say."

As he dove into his third whiskey, I said, "Have you ever heard about big cats that can stand up on their hind legs?"

He nearly choked, and then started laughing in a hoarse cackle. "Not that old story again. Come on, Quatermain. You must have heard the stories, about the *imbulu*. People who have been cursed. Or animals who have been cursed. Or devils. They show up, tempt people, cause problems. Never saw anything like it myself, but I've heard the locals talking. A lot of rubbish, if you ask me. There's even supposed to be an *imbulu* tribe, hidden away somewhere. Pure fairy tale stuff. Just old legends to frighten us away."

"I thought the *imbulu* were lizard creatures," I said, convinced Pruet had his myths confused.

He looked puzzled. "Really? I recall something about them turning into humans. One disguised itself as a princess and tried to marry a prince, but couldn't get rid of its tail. That was a lizard? Honestly, I get these folk tales mixed up. Then maybe it's a *tokoloshe*."

"Those are bear-like. I mean something that looks like a panther."

"I recall some old story from the Congo, but can't remember the details," he said. "Too long ago. Maybe you've discovered a new species."

"Hardly," I said. Although perhaps someone else had discovered a creature never before seen and was using it to help abduct natives for the slave trade.

The mention of the Congo made me recalled the darts the creature had used from its blowgun in Umgibeli's kraal, one felling Mnqoba, putting him asleep for hours. The blowgun were often used in the Congo by...

I dropped my fork.

"I say, old man," Pruet said, "you look as though you've seen a ghost. All this rot about *imbulu* has got you spooked."

I remembered the feathered dart that had been used against Mnqoba. I also remembered seeing one similar. When I was about to enter Blake's house to turn in for the night. One of those darts had struck me. I had pulled it free and looked at it just before I fell unconscious. But something more had been on that dart, some sort of poison. Not something that would kill me, as they had killed the chieftains and their witch doctors. Not an anesthetic as was used on Mnqoba and those that were captured and carried away. But something that put me into a state of unconsciousness and provided me with symptoms of fever.

The slavers had attacked Blake and Emma's house!

I felt such a fool. Here I was, in the safety of Durban, while Emma Cairns was in danger. But that had been many days ago. She could be dead, or have been carried away with the others abducted. I needed to get back there. I needed to find out what happened.

Mnqoba had to have been the one who brought me back to Durban for medical attention. Why he hadn't stayed at my house or come back to check on my recovery, I did not know. I had to find him.

My meal had revived me. I was regaining my strength, now it was time to regain my lost days.

Mnqoba had no family. He had been orphaned, which was how he had been part of my father's mission long ago. He did have many cousins, or those he claimed were cousins. I did not know any specifically, since he had always rattled off names and places, each one always different from the last. So I went to those I knew who might know him. These were men whom I had used at times on hunting trips in the time before Solomon's mines. First I went to the merchants that outfitted expeditions. Men were often hired through them. But Mnqoba was not known to any of them. Then I went to more unofficial labor exchanges, where locals gathered to gossip.

"Greetings, Macumazahn," said one old gentleman smoking a cigarette under a tree with half a dozen younger men. "Do you plan another trip?"

They all looked at me hopefully. They were all dressed in worn trousers and shirts, some with sandals. I recognized some faces but couldn't place names to them, except the old man, who had been on a few of my trips in the past.

"Greetings, Siphiwe," I said. "No, not right now."

The faces of the young men fell into disappointment.

"I'm looking for Mnqoba," I said. "He was on my last trip and I need to pay him. Do you know him?"

"I know him," said one man. "Give me the money and I will give it to him."

The other men laughed at him, even Siphiwe. The man looked sheepish for a moment, then laughed himself.

"I know Mnqoba," Siphiwe said, "but I have not seen him for many days."

"You could try Malusi's daughter," said one of the men. "He was always trying to court her."

The others laughed again at this, and another said, "Everyone is trying to court her. She is beautiful, but Mnqoba has no prospects and she and everyone else have turned him down."

"She turned you down, too," chastised the first man.

He shrugged and replied, "I have no prospects either. And neither do you."

"True," said the first. "But she didn't turn me down."

"Because you didn't try to court her, or she would have."

"True. I never tried. She is too far above me."

"My sister is too far above you!"

Siphiwe looked at me and shook his head. "Ntombikayise, who sells fruit from her garden, may have seen him. She may be his aunt. Or friends to an aunt."

I asked where I should find this Ntombikayise, and he directed me to one of the markets on the other side of Durban. I thanked Siphiwe with some coins and told him to treat all the men with him to a meal, but no drink. After all, I could afford to be generous and was now in a position to help out these men. But I was no fool. Had I given money to each, some of them would have gotten drunk rather than had a meal. That is the way of some of the idle poor, whether in London or Durban.

I hired another rickshaw to carry me to the market Siphiwe had indicated. As it was later in the day, many of the stalls were empty. I did not hold out much hope of finding the woman, but had no other choice.

I asked a few vendors closing down, and they pointed me in the right direction.

Ntombikayise was a heavy set, middle aged woman sitting in the shade of her stall, fanning herself. The stall was a rickety affair of saplings holding up a blanket to keep the sun off of her and her table of produce. There was a sad collection of vegetables on the table. When she saw me approach, a huge smile widened her features, forming dimples in her fat cheeks.

"Welcome, *inkosi*. You wish to buy some delicious vegetables? The finest in Natal."

"I wish to find Mnqoba," I said. "I was told you were his aunt."

"Ah, well, he calls me that. He sometimes live with the son of my sister, whom he calls cousin, so he thinks we are related. What has he done now?"

"Nothing," I said. "We were just on a trip together and I want to make sure he is all right."

She lost her smile and eyed me from under heavy brows. "And why would you want to know this?"

"I'm his friend."

She snorted. "White man a friend to a black man?" she said as though I had just stated that it was raining strudel. "He stole something from you, and you wish to punish him."

"No. I really am his friend. I hired him for a hunting trip, and I have not seen him since we came back. I've known him since he was little. My father taught him at the mission. I am called Macumazahn by…"

She jumped up. "Macumazahn! Watcher-by-Night! Why did you not say so? I know of you, Macumazahn. Somehow," she looked me up and down, "I thought you would be taller."

"And younger," I said.

She shook her head. "No. I knew you would be old."

I frowned at her choice of words.

"You have been known since the time of Mpande. You are a friend to the Zulu people."

"Have you seen Mnqoba?" I asked, interrupting her before she went through a long history I had no desire to relive.

"No. Go see my nephew, Khulekani."

I sighed wearily. "Where can I find him?"

She told me and I chose the most decrepit yam on her table, paying her enough for all of her produce. When I was out of sight, I tossed the yam aside and called for yet another rickshaw.

Her directions brought me to an area outside Durban not far from my own bungalow. Khulekani's one-room clapboard house was small, not much more than a shack, one of many clustered together. Evening was approaching as I arrived to find a young woman pulling vegetables from the garden beside the house. A cooking fire in front heated a small cast iron pot of water which was beginning to boil.

When the woman stood up, her hands loaded with gem squash destined for the pot, I saw that her belly protruded in the early months of pregnancy.

"Good evening, *nkosikazi*," I said. "Is this the home of Khulekani?"

She eyed me suspiciously and walked to the fire, dropping the gem squash into the boiling water. When she was done, she lowered her eyes and gave a curt response.

"He is not here, *inkosi*."

"I have just come from his aunt, Ntombikayise," I began.

She looked at me suddenly. "Has something happened to her?"

"No. She's fine. I have come looking for Mnqoba. I understand that he and Khulekani are friends or cousins."

She shook her head. "He is not here."

Presently a tall, broad shouldered man walked up to the house. He was rough looking, in his middle thirties, with heavily muscled arms and thickly callused hands. He was dressed in trousers and a shirt with the sleeves rolled up to his bulging biceps, and a pair of old brogans. When he saw me talking to the woman his face darkened, but after the initial glare, he lowered his eyes. His jaw remained tight and the muscles of his arms twitched.

"He is looking for Mnqoba," the woman said quickly.

"My name's Quatermain," I said.

He looked up at me in surprise, suspicion and anger evaporating. "Macumazahn? You are Macumazahn, friend to Mnqoba?"

"Yes," I said.

The woman placed her hand over her open mouth in surprise.

Khulekani bowed his head. "Mnqoba has told me much about the great Macumazahn. I am honored."

"Don't believe everything Mnqoba tells you. He tends to exaggerate. We were on a hunting trip recently, and I became ill. I was in fever all through our return, so I'm looking for Mnqoba to find out what happened during the hunt and to pay him for his services. Have you seen him?"

Khulekani shook his head. "I saw him after a trip with you several days ago. He said a white man died on the hunt, but did not tell me more.

Something bothered him from that trip. Then he left again. He said Macumazahn needed him. That was all. We have not seen him since."

"Yes, we did have a tragic hunt. Then I was going back out, and he ended up joining me. But you haven't seen him since we've been back? It's only been a day or so. Could he have gone to stay with someone else?"

"Yes, but not likely. He has no home of his own. My wife, Sizani, is actually his cousin, so he often stays with us. He calls me cousin. He gives us money he earns on hunting trips, although I tell him not to, that he must save it for his own family some day. I work loading ships at Durban Harbor, but even that is not enough. He helps us as often as he can. He said he wants to be godfather to our first born, but I do not know what that means."

I looked at the woman and smiled. "It means he greatly honors your child."

They both smiled in return and she caressed her swollen belly.

I left them and dragged my exhausted body toward my house. If Mnqoba did not return to his cousin and Khulekani, where did he go? And if he never came back, how did I return to Durban and where was Mnqoba now?

CHAPTER ELEVEN

Mortimer stood at my door the next morning.

"Well, you are looking better, Mr. Quatermain. It seems that Kaya's ministering is helping you gain your strength back. I hope you are getting along well together. I am assured that she is an excellent nurse."

"Well enough," I said.

I never bothered to mention my travels of the previous day, the hearty meal, or the good night's sleep, up before dawn, a brisk walk and a good breakfast. Although still a bit weak, I was beginning to feel like my old self.

"Good of you to drop by, Mortimer," I said, for I had determined to approach him or someone else at the Colonial Office. This business was becoming serious and needed intervention, and I did not give him the opportunity to enter the house but pulled shut the door and confronted him on the little veranda. "Can you tell me who brought me back to Durban?"

"I'm afraid I wasn't present. I assumed it was your man that went on the trip with you, I forget his name. He dropped you off here, sent for a doctor, and took your wagon and oxen. Sorry to say that he sold the animals and the wagon. Probably kept the money. You know how those people are."

I bristled at this. "Mnqoba went with me, and a more trusting and loyal man you will never find. I don't believe he was the one who brought me back. No one has seen him for several days."

"Exactly. He took your money and has gone. I will put in an official inquiry and investigate this incident. We'll find the man, don't worry, Mr. Quatermain."

"I am concerned," I said to him in a sharp tone, "because Mnqoba and I have uncovered slave trading going on along the Transvaal broader. Kraals have been raided and people abducted."

"This is a serious accusation, Mr. Quatermain. Do you have any idea who is behind this?"

"No. I was visiting a farm owned by Dr. Emerson Blake and Emma Cairns. We were at the kraal of Umgibeli. Slavers have attacked another kraal in the area. We foiled their plans at this kraal and found that white men were involved. The closest were Blake and Mrs. Cairns, so Umgibeli's people planned to raid their farm. Mnqoba and I went first, to investigate who might be living there, since it had been a Boer farm that had been abandoned. Blake's a retired physician and Mrs. Cairns is the wife of his late partner and they have nothing to do with the slave trade. I would have gone to Umgibeli's kraal next morning to dissuade the warriors from attacking, but I was made unconscious and fell sick. We need to get to Blake's farm if it isn't already too late."

"You were made unconscious, you say?"

"Yes. One of those blowgun darts some of the Congo tribes use, dipped in some anesthetic. The slavers use them to abduct their victims a few at a time. They also use poisoned ones to kill the chiefs of the kraals they raid, to put the people into a state of fear and confusion."

"Amazing," Mortimer said.

"So you see," I insisted, "Blake and Mrs. Cairns are in danger on two fronts. The slavers were already there, and Umgibeli's warriors were on their way."

Mortimer laughed. I had expected some sort of display of concern from him, but not humor. Obviously he was ridiculing me, treating these as fevered imaginations.

"Look, Mortimer, if you aren't going to take this seriously, I know others in the colonial government who will."

"Of course you do," he said, quickly gaining his composure. "I know you have many important friends, Mr. Quatermain, which is why we have been paying so close attention to you. Do you think every trader or hunter who comes back from the bush gets the treatment you have received? We are aware of your connections, your friendship with Sir Henry Curtis, and your importance in general. We are concerned for your safety."

"I'm of no importance, Mortimer, when there is an innocent woman's life at stake."

"Calm yourself, sir. All is well. When you went back into the bush, we sent some soldiers after you in the hopes of preventing you from falling into the same fate as your friend, Mr. Kennedy. They have only just returned with word that an incident with the locals has been avoided. Apparently the appearance of a dozen of Her Majesty's finest, armed to the teeth, put the fear of God into them. As Blake's is the only white settlement in that area, they have garrisoned there for a few days and sent a messenger back with word. Unfortunately, they had missed you and your man on your way back to Natal. Or I should say fortunately, since if they came across you first, they would have escorted you to the nearest safe place for medical help and never reached Blake's farm, and those devils might have followed through with their threat. But rest assured, all are safe. Your man might have sent a message to the Zulus, or he stopped at that village before bringing you here."

"Or Zakhele went back to his people and told them Blake and Emma Cairns were innocent. He was with Mnqoba and me. What about the slavers?" I asked.

"No sign of them. The messenger never mentioned slavers, only that you had been taken ill and your man took you back to Natal before they had arrived. But if I were you, I would not mention anything more about slavers. As it is, our peace with Transvaal is a precarious one. Still some sour grapes about them gaining their independence. If we let out that some Boers are crossing the boarder to raid villages, public opinion might turn against the new state and another war might start. Keep this under your hat until we can do a proper investigation. I'll make certain it is done discreetly, so the Boers don't get wind of it. If their government is involved, then we can deal with it through diplomatic channels."

I sank into one of the old wicker chairs on the veranda. It creaked under me. I felt the worries of the past day lifting off of me.

Mortimer patted my shoulder. "You see, Mr. Quatermain. Nothing to worry about. All has been taken care off. Because of you, some innocent people have been spared and now we know to hunt down some trespassing slavers. Now all you have to do is gain back your strength so you can return to England. I'm sure your friends and your son are anxious for your return."

He left me then with a contented feeling that those people on that little farm were safe. I had known Emma Cairns for a few short hours but I had grown fond of her. She had already seen too much tragedy in her life; she did not need to have more with a raid from Dumisani and his warriors or from slavers. Perhaps I could visit her place before I left Africa. I would be my old self in a day or so. At the very least, I could write to her to let her know that I had recovered. I could send someone trusted with the letter to deliver it.

Which brought my thoughts to Mnqoba.

I would have believed I knew his character well enough to know that he would not have sold my oxen and wagon, and leave with the money. He could have deposited the money in my account in the Durban bank. I would have to check, for I could not see Mnqoba as a thief. Nor would he take the money and run away with it. Where would he go? He did not drink alcohol and he did not gamble. Those vices never had any influence over him. Nor had the pursuit of women, although he did have his share of romances. He had lamented that he lacked cattle to offer for the hand of Liyana, but she was a chief's daughter and exceptional. If Liyana had not been one of those abducted, I could suspect him of using my money to buy cattle. But she was gone, and he had no place of his own to keep cattle. Could he have been so taken by the chief's daughter that he had gone off on his own to rescue her? I could not see him doing this by himself, but perhaps he had some clue as to where the slavers were going that forced him not to delay. After all, I had been unconscious for several days, thanks to these slavers. He might have discovered something I was unaware of. But he should have left a message for me.

I went through my things that had been piled near the door and could find nothing. There was nothing anywhere in the house.

If he intended to return and hunt for Liyana, why would he sell the wagon and oxen instead of using them? I could only guess that he bought a horse and some supplies with the money and set off in pursuit in this manner.

There are a few merchants on the outside of Durban who equipped expeditions, built or repaired wagons, and handled ox and horses, and one in particular that I usually dealt with. De Vries & Co. had been established in the 30s and now was under the management of the third generation,

Ambroos. Kennedy and I had started our hunting trip from Maritzburg, so I had dealt with the De Vries & Company there; but if Mnqoba had sold our wagon and team after brining me to Durban, he most likely brought them to the Durban branch. When Kaya came to my house that morning to attend to me, I shooed her away and insisted I was fine. She argued, and I left her in her combative state on my veranda as I headed down the street in the direction of Durban proper. I took a rickshaw, which carried me to the establishment of De Vries & Co.

Ambroos de Vries was in a state of irritation, lamenting over the expansion of the railroad and the demise of the wagon industry. He was dressed in a leather apron, shirt sleeves rolled back, with a wooden mallet in his hand as he worked on repairing a wagon with a younger apprentice.

"*Heer* Quatermain!" he said when he saw me, tossed his mallet aside, and immediately grabbed my hand in both of his and began pumping it. "So good to see you, sir. You don't look well. Have you been ill?"

"Touch of fever," I said.

"Come into the office, my friend. I will have tea prepared."

He took me aside, called to the apprentice to bring tea, and guided me into the hot office with windows wide to allow a warm breeze to alleviate the stuffiness and rustle the piles of papers. As we sat over tea in decorative china cups, I inquired over his father's health. The older de Vries had retired a few years earlier, leaving the business in the hands of his eldest son, who was not yet forty.

"I heard a rumor that you had retired and had moved to England," he said.

"A nasty rumor," I said. "But mostly true. I came back for a little hunting trip."

"So you be wanting a wagon and team, then."

"Actually, no. We've already done the trip, out of Maritzburg."

"Not that crooked Portuguese," he said.

"No, your place in Maritzburg."

"As long as it wasn't that Portuguese. I hope Kristoffer took good care of you. So, what can I do for you? Have you come to complain about my little brother?"

"No. He treated us fine. Do you remember Mnqoba the Zulu? He went with me on that trip. When I took ill, he brought me back. He sold the wagon and team and then disappeared."

"Ah, and you want the scoundrel caught and punished."

"No, I want to find out where he's gotten to. I'm afraid he might be in danger."

De Vries furrowed his heavy brows at me and shook his head. "I will never understand you, *Heer* Quatermain. Still, what can I do?"

"Knowing Mnqoba, he would have brought the wagon back to you. Now, I believe he was heading back into Zululand alone. He might have purchased a horse…"

De Vries held up his hand to interrupt me. "No, I'm afraid he did not come here. We bought a wagon a few days ago, but that was through a European. An Irishman, I'm thinking. No black man has brought us so much as a single ox in months. I'm sorry *Heer* Quatermain, but perhaps your man has taken the wagon for his own use or sold it elsewhere. I know this Mnqoba enough to recognize him, so he may not have wanted me to know he was selling your property."

"Mnqoba isn't like that," I insisted.

De Vries gave me a condescending look, as though I was very naive. "I'm sorry I can't help you."

I finished the last bit of tea and stood up. "Thank you for your time anyway, *Heer* de Vries." Then the thought struck me that Blake himself might have brought me back, then gotten rid of the wagon and team under Mnqoba's instructions.

"The European who brought in the wagon," I said, "are you certain he was Irish? Could he have been a learned Englishman in his late fifties?"

"No, he was in his forties. Rough looking man. He might have been a hunter or mercenary, but certainly not a trader. And his accent was Irish or Welsh, or even Scots."

"So he wasn't a Boer?" I asked, thinking of Blake's hired men.

"*God in de Hemel*, no! Wouldn't you think I would recognize a Boer? He was Irish, or whatever, and not someone who has lived most of his life in Africa, as you have. Although he has been here a while, if his clothes were any indication. Shabby, if you ask me. Old hat, with a Zebra pelt around it. Totally disreputable looking."

One of the men who had tried to follow Mnqoba and me, whom we thought we had lost on the veldt. I had given them little thought since the day we had left them behind, with their horses on the run and their boots up a thorn tree. How did they get their hands on a wagon? Was it mine?

"May I see this wagon?" I asked.

He nodded, concerned over the change in my expression. He knew something bothered me and he hurried to show me to the rear of his establishment. In the yard behind the building, next to the kraals for cattle and horses, sat two wagons. One was in need of repair, the other in fairly good condition. One wagon is pretty much like another, yet each is unique. Different makers have different styles and designs. Wear upon them is different. And even though some may look alike, there are subtle differences in the feel. I climbed onto the box from which the team would be driven. I ran my hands over the scratches in the wood, grasped the brake handle and pulled it. Yes, I had spent the past few weeks on this wagon. This had carried Mnqoba and I to the kraals of Umgibeli and Izoqa, and then to Blake's homestead.

If Mnqoba had brought me back from Blake's farm in this wagon, how did the Irishman get possession of it to sell it to de Vries? Mnqoba could have run across these two on his return toward Durban, but why would he give them the wagon? Perhaps he convinced them to take me for medical help while he returned to search for Liyana. Their payment for such a deed would be the sale of the wagon and team. I could not see Mnqoba entrusting my welfare to the hands of strangers who had been pursuing us under mysterious circumstances. I could understand his urgency to find Liyana, but this whole scenario made no sense. Furthermore, Mortimer had told me it was Mnqoba who had brought me back. And I had seen Mortimer interact briefly with these two men after our first meeting. There was something more complicated in the works. My greatest concern, though, was Mnqoba's whereabouts? If he did not bring me back to Durban, where was he? More than likely when I was laid low and taken ill by the slaver's poisoned dart, he went after the slavers to rescue Liyana. Blake was a doctor, though retired. He still had a facility in the one building where he might treat the people that worked for him or even some local natives who needed medical attention. Mnqoba would have no fear of leaving me in Blake's capable hands. But how did I get from Blake's farm to Durban, and how did those two shady characters get their hands on my wagon?

And why had Mortimer lied?

CHAPTER TWELVE

My immediate inclination was to return to Blake and Emma's homestead. I would find the answers to most of my questions there. I could also pursue Mnqoba, so that he would not tackle these slavers on his own, if indeed that is what he did. My concern was that I was over a week and many miles behind him. I would never be able to catch up with him, but I might be able to help in some way. I could not sit still while the young Zulu faced unknown dangers to rescue a woman he hardly knew. He was motivated by some romantic interest, rescuing the damsel in distress. Perhaps he believed that if he rescued her he could win her heart and her hand, though he was but a poor, homeless man. But I thought better of Mnqoba and believed he would brave dangers because it was necessary to fight an evil.

Perhaps that was the evil Izula had meant when she had made her mysterious visit to my house. I could not let Mnqoba face it alone. More than likely, if he was not killed outright, he would be taken as a slave. I could at least track him, find the slavers, and see to their downfall. At least bringing in the authorities, since I am an old man who has passed his prime and long ago left those days of righting wrongs all by himself. Also, facing a band of slavers was not my idea of something I could accomplish on my own. I am not a brave man. Still, I could not abandon Mnqoba.

I purchased two horses from de Vries and the necessary supplies, to use one horse as a pack animal. Then I hired a rickshaw to return to my house to gather some items, particularly some of my guns.

Mortimer was sitting on my veranda when I arrived.

"Ah, Mister Quatermain! Good to see you up and about. Getting some exercise, I see."

"Yes. Feeling much better, thank you. No need to concern yourself any longer."

"Oh, no problem at all. So, I imagine you will be ready to return to England at the earliest opportunity."

"Eventually," I said.

"I'm afraid that every moment you delay your return puts you at risk."

"Risk? What sort of risk?"

"The slavers, of course. You single-handedly exposed an on-going slave trade along the border territory. Don't you think that some of their agents would look forward to removing you as an obstacle? Your testimony will bring action against them. They would stop at nothing to silence you."

"That's ridiculous," I said. "I have no evidence and I can make no statement other than people are being abducted. I saw no one and could identify no one. All that's up to you people. Send in troops. Perform an investigation. Obviously that's the sort of thing for the colonial government to deal with. I merely brought it to your attention. My involvement is done."

"Exactly! Therefore, there is no reason for you to remain in Natal. A ship will be leaving tomorrow for Cape Town, and another from Cape Town to England. I have already booked passage for you, at the expense of Her Majesty's government in appreciation for all that you have done."

"That's rather presumptuous of you, Mr. Mortimer," I said, bristling. "I have business to attend to here in Durban."

"For your own safety, Mr. Quatermain, I must insist. Any business can be handled through your solicitor. I can have him brought over later, or you can send instructions to him through a letter. For the time being, I suggest you rest. That woman, Kaya I believe her name is, will be here shortly and will help you pack up your belongings for the voyage."

"Mr. Mortimer," I began, indignant, my jaw straining as I made an attempt to control my sudden rage, "you have overstepped your authority. I shall be speaking to your superiors about this impertinence."

"I have the full support of Governor Bulwer," he said. "He realizes your importance and wishes you to return to the safety of England as soon as possible."

He turned to greet two men approaching the house. I had heard their footsteps, but my anger at the colonial officer forced me to ignore them. When I followed Mortimer's gaze, I found the same two men who had followed Mnqoba and me and who had sold my wagon and oxen to de Vries.

"These are my two agents," Mortimer said. "Mr. Finnegan and Mr. Pepper." He indicated the man in the hat with the Zebra pelt band first.

"These are government agents?" I asked.

"Yes," Mortimer said. "They work exclusively for me. They were sent after you when you went back into the bush in order to protect you. They lost you a few days out, but eventually found you at Dr. Blake's homestead. They brought you back, after Blake did what he could for you. My apologies for deceiving you, but I did not want their involvement known."

"So you let me believe that Mnqoba brought me back and told me he stole from me."

"It was a believable story. Those natives are always ready to rob anyone

"Send in troops. Perform an investigation."

blind. You should know that for as long as you have had dealings with them."

I indeed had the opposite view because of my long history with the indigenous people of Africa.

"Where is Mnqoba?" I demanded.

"I'm sure I don't know. These gentlemen did not run across him at Blake's farm. Certainly he abandoned you. And fortunately for you, my men were there to bring you back safe and sound. Now, you may return home."

"Why don't you just bring in a platoon of colonial troops in here to force me to leave?" I said.

"Do you really want that? Actually, the Governor thought it best to keep everything low keyed. We do not want to draw any unnecessary attention to you, yet the Governor wants you protected. These two men have served Her Majesty for many years and have held army commissions. I trust them implicitly."

Mortimer motioned to the front door. "Please, Mr. Quatermain. It's for your own safety and the good of the empire."

Considering that Mortimer's agents were armed and I was not, both were at least ten years my juniors, and that I was still very weak from my recent ordeal, I believed discretion the better part of valor. I entered my house, slamming the door in Mortimer's face.

The first thing I noticed was that my rifles were gone. I found my revolver and holster where I had left them in the bedroom, where Mortimer never thought to look, and put them on. Then I stuffed my pipe, sat down, and boiled.

My angry ruminations were interrupted an hour later by someone knocking at the door. I pulled the door open with the intention of a verbal assault upon Mortimer or one of his men, to demand my lawyer at once, to see the governor himself, and to many other stipulations I had conjured up over that hour. Kaya's large eye met me on the other side of a wooden bowl draped with a towel and smelling suspiciously like stew. I motioned her inside and the fear that had washed over her faded to mere apprehension.

Before I shut the door, I noticed Mr. Finnegan and Mr. Pepper seated on my wicker chairs, smoking foul smelling cigars. If they are to smoke, at least they should have the decency to not smoke the cheep tobacco.

I led the trembling woman to the dining table, where she placed the bowl down and pulled off the towel.

"Will you join me?" I asked as I retrieved a ladle, bowls and spoons from the kitchen.

"No, *inkosi*," she said, her voice shaky. "That would not be proper."

Nevertheless, I filled both bowls and set one in front of her, motioning for her to sit down. "It smells delicious," I said. "I'm afraid I was rather harsh to you yesterday. Forgive me, Kaya."

She nodded and lifted a spoon full of stew to her lips.

"Who are those men outside, *inkosi*?" she asked before she put the spoon in her mouth.

I sat opposite her and ate a spoonful before answering her, for I was starving. She followed suit.

"They are men working for the colonial agent Mortimer," I said. "They are supposedly here for my protection. Why?"

"I have seen them before, in Dr. McKinny's office. I believe they asked the doctor to see you at your home, before I was sent for. You asked me to ask the doctor who had sent for him, but he would not tell me. It was none of my business, he said. But seeing them here, also, makes me believe that it was them that sent the doctor to you. There was no one else to his office except patients that day."

"Yes," I said. "That makes sense. Apparently they are the ones who brought me back to Durban from Zululand."

"Then they are friends of yours?" she asked doubtfully.

"Certainly not. They intend to hold me here until the boat to Cape Town is ready to sail. And they'll probably go along to make certain I get on the steamer for England at Cape Town."

"Do you not want to return to England?"

"Not yet. Not until I find out the fate of my friend, Mnqoba."

"The Zulu man? You call him friend?"

"Yes. And he would not leave me in a pickle, I certainly won't leave him in one."

"But he is black."

"So are you," I pointed out. "So are most of the people in Natal."

"But you call him friend?"

"Yes. We have known each other a long time. Now look, Kaya, do you want to help me?"

"If I can, *inkosi*."

I gave her instructions, had her repeat them to me, then sent her on her way after the stew was gone.

The next morning, Finnegan pushed open my front door and informed me that it was time to catch the boat to Cape Town. He was not a reasonable person to begin with, but after an evening of fitfully dozing on chairs on my veranda, he and his partner were positively mean. The wicker furniture makes a nice pastime, but a whole night on them makes a sore back. Add to that the feasting of insects. Finnegan's hand rested on the pistol holstered at his side, as if the threat was not obvious.

I wore my own revolver now, and was sorely tempted to shoot both of them, but that would only land me in jail until the issue could be investigated. I could not allow my departure to be delayed any longer, so I had to trust that others would follow through with my plea for help.

I was escorted to the Durban docks where we found the steamship, *Song of Solomon*. I carried only a bag with changes of clothes and a few personal articles. Finnegan and Pepper, both smelling foul from their restless night and in even fouler moods, pushed me along, making empty threats punctuated with curses. Neither of them had forgotten the trick Mnqoba had played upon them, tossing their boots into a mimosa tree, and they still bore the marks to remind them. They remarked graphically what they would do to Mnqoba if they ever found him, which was unlikely to happen if I knew my friend as well as I did.

My cabin on the *Song* was small and stuffy, but the trip would be short. Apparently both men had also booked passage, to make certain I was on the steamer that left Cape Town for Portsmouth. I would do my best to disappoint them, even if it came down to shooting both men. Not to kill them, mind you, but to incapacitate them. I was not about to leave Africa, no matter what. If my plan, with Kaya's help, was not fulfilled, then I had to turn to drastic means.

The boat's whistle sounded and I felt the engines turn over through the vibrations in the deck. I had only moments left, and my secondary plan seemed the most likely. It was distasteful for me, though I had little fear that I could wound both men before they had the opportunity to draw their weapons, but shooting to wound is still a risky business.

I moved my hand to my revolver, just as there came a knock on the cabin door.

Finnegan opened the door and received a huge fist in the nose.

My revolver was out of its holster and shoved into the neck of Pepper.

"Do not move," I said, very calmly and very seriously.

Pepper lifted his hands and I relieved him of his gun.

Khulekani stepped through the door, barely fitting through the frame, and struck Finnegan again. The man's knees buckled and he dropped to the deck.

Three other stevedores pushed their way into the cramped cabin, one taking Finnegan's revolver and two taking hold of Pepper.

"Tie them up nicely," I said.

Khulekani grinned as he pulled lengths of rope from his pockets. "We came prepared for that. Now you go, Macumazahn, and find Mnqoba. We will see that these two go on a nice voyage and do not bother you."

"You are making a mistake, Quatermain," Pepper said.

He did not elaborate as one of Khulekani's companions struck him heavily in the mouth, loosening at least one tooth.

"Do not speak to Macumazahn in that way!" the man said.

I grabbed my bag of belongings and left Mr. Finnegan and Mr. Pepper in the capable hands of Khulekani and his companions. They would see that the two agents were securely bound, left in the cabin, and would make the voyage to Cape Town in my stead. They might be found by the time they reach their destination, or some time afterwards. I would be long gone, on horseback and on my way to Blake's homestead.

Chapter Thirteen

My trip back was uneventful yet filled with worry and apprehension. Mortimer had told me that all were safe and sound, but I could not trust him. He had tried to force me to return to England. He had lied about Mnqoba. No telling what else he had lied about. I did not believe for an instant that he was trying to protect me. I may know some influential people, but I am no one of consequence. I'm an old hunter, nothing more. And so I had no idea what I would find at Blake and Emma's farm. The place could be a pile of ashes, Dumisani having followed through with his threat and attacked in retaliation for the deaths and abductions, even though Emma and Blake had nothing to do with them. Or the slavers, who had poisoned me, killed everyone before Dumisani even had the chance to attack.

My heart was in turmoil. I did not know Emma Cairns well, as we had only brief conversations over a few shared hours, but she was a fine, intelligent, likable woman who had gone through tragedies with which I could sympathize. I had no desire to develop a deeper relationship. I was past any interest in romance. But I did not want to see any harm befall her. Perhaps I could even take her back to England with me, to help her begin a new life. I had plenty of money, thanks to our exploits at Solomon's mines, so I could easily devote some small bit of my fortune in helping someone with a good heart.

Provided she was still alive.

And what of Mnqoba? Possibly he was attacked by the same scoundrels who had used the dart on me and was either unconscious, ill, or dead. Or the slavers had taken him north with the others they had abducted, or he was in pursuit of those slavers in some quixotic attempt to rescue Liyana.

Too many question, too many possibilities, I was driving myself insane. Days and nights of these thoughts, I was going mad.

Imagine my relief when I crested a hill and saw Blake's farm, as peaceful as it had been when I had first seen it.

As I approached, both I and my horses weary of the long, hastened ride, Blake came out upon the veranda, shotgun in hand. Then he called into the house, and after a moment Emma joined him.

Emma ran up to meet me, her pretty face split with a wide grin. "Allan! I thought I'd never see you again. I've been so worried about you, you were so sick when you left."

I dropped from my horse and faced her. "I've been worried about you, too."

"Me? Whatever for?"

"We can discuss that after I've taken care of the horses," I said.

"Kuan-yin will take care of them," she said. "You look awful. You need to sit down and have a good meal. You must be exhausted."

Blake took the reins to my horses and called out for Kuan-yin. I took one of my bundles from the pack horse and Emma encircled my arm with hers and guided me to the veranda.

"What about Mnqoba?" I asked. "Where is he?"

She gave a glance to Blake before saying, "One of the natives you came with? I'm sure I don't know. They both took off after you fell ill. We haven't seen them since. We suspected them of making you sick, since they left so quickly."

"That would never be the case," I said. Especially with Mnqoba. More than likely he and Zakhele returned to Umgibeli's kraal to prevent Dumisani from attacking the homestead. Mnqoba may have found the dart that had poisoned me and gone in search of the slavers either by himself, with Zakhele, or with Dumisani's aid. Now that I knew Emma was safe, I could rest and head to Umgibeli's kraal.

Emma took me to the spare room I had used previously, though briefly. She summoned Jiaying to bring me a basin of fresh water. Once washed, I changed into clean yet wrinkled clothes from the bundle I had taken from the horse. I felt years younger, though I suppose the relief at finding Emma and Blake well and out of danger had more to do with it than cleaning up and putting on fresh clothes. My only concern was Mnqoba.

Although they had already eaten, Emma had Jiaying prepare some cold meats for me. It was past mid day and I had not eaten since that morning, breakfasting on some biltong. I was famished.

Emma sat with me in the dining room, sipping some wine, while Blake was off seeing to other matters. He was not happy over my return, though he played the most gracious of hosts. I still felt he experienced a certain amount of jealousy toward me because of Emma's exuberant attention, but he needn't feel so threatened. I was here only briefly and I offered Emma some slight diversion to the boredom she might feel being stranded in the wilderness.

"Why did you come back so soon, Allan?" she asked. "I mean, I had hoped you would come back for a visit, but it has only been a week. You were deathly ill when they took you away. Emerson did what he could for you, treating you with quinine, but he thought it best if you received other help, perhaps even a hospital stay. Emerson's expertise does not include tropical diseases and we aren't equipped to handle such emergencies here. You should have stayed in Durban and rested before you attempted to journey back here. Not that I'm not pleased you did. I flatter myself to think that you risked your health to see me."

She flushed a little, looking down into her wine glass.

"You," I said, "and to determine Mnqoba's fate."

Her eyes flashed. "Your servant?"

"He's no servant. He is my friend and I need to find out what happened to him. He would not willingly desert me, especially if I had fallen ill."

"He's a black man," she said, her words tight, her features darker. "They cannot be trusted."

I thought of the loss of her son at Isandlwana at the hands of the Zulu and decided it better not to argue at the moment about the qualities of men, white or black.

"If you don't mind," I said, "might I stay the night to allow my horses to rest before I go on to Umgibeli's kraal?"

The darkness fled from her face, replaced by disappointment. "I was hoping you would stay longer."

"Not while a slave trade is operating in this area. When I succumbed to sickness, who found me?"

"Pieter, who was doing his rounds as our lookout. He found you collapsed on the veranda."

"And did anyone find a small feathered dart?"

Her brow furrowed in puzzlement. "No. Why?"

"Because I was struck by a dart similar to those used by the slavers to abduct natives from their kraals. Probably the very same way they killed the chiefs and witch doctors. I may have been poisoned, either the dose was incorrect to kill me or I removed the dart in time. Or I may have had a reaction to their choice in anesthetics. In any case, that is how I became sick. My worry was that the slavers came through here and could have killed all of you."

She stared at me over the brim of her wine glass. "You believe we are still in danger?"

"Probably not. Your man Pieter may have frightened them away. You are more secure than a typical homestead. They may just keep clear of here from now on. I'd suggest letting your men know so they could double their efforts in guarding the place at night."

"I'll tell Josef right away," she said.

"There's also another matter I'd like to ask you about," I began, not sure how to broach this subject.

One side of her mouth curled up as she tilted her head. "Oh?"

I was afraid she may have gotten the wrong impression and I felt momentarily uncomfortable. "Ah, this may sound strange, but have you or any of your people seen any unusual animals around lately?"

She set her glass down and lean on the table, arms crossed. "Unusual, how?"

"Large cats, like panthers, that have the ability to walk upright."

She laughed outright, and I felt even more uncomfortable.

"Really, Allan. You were in a state of fever. I don't think you should rely on anything you saw while in fever."

"No, this wasn't during the fever, this was before, and I was not the only person to see them."

"Them? More than one?"

"An American and I were hunting, and he was attacked and eventually died. It was a large panther that had the ability to stand upright on two legs. I was able to wound it but was unable to chase it down because of the American's wounds. He died later at a nearby kraal."

"Oh, how terrible."

"When Mnqoba and I learned of the abductions at another kraal, we set a trap for the kidnappers. One of those involved was more man-like than animal, but still panther-like in the head and face. It may just have been a disguise, but it seems such a strange coincidence. I was wondering if there were some species of panther yet to be discovered."

"That hardly seems likely," she said, becoming very serious and analytical, "considering the vast differences between the two creatures. You say the first was a panther with human-like characteristics to make it able to walk on hind legs, yet the second was man-like with panther characteristics. Have you read Darwin? Or Galton? No? Well, this just doesn't fit into the scheme of the evolution of life. I could possibly see that these might be different degrees of evolutionary changes from an actual panther to a human, but humans share their evolution with the great apes, not the big cats. No, if what you saw was real, they may not be natural, or they were tricks played upon you. Like you suggested, disguises. Perhaps to frighten the natives. They are a superstitious lot."

"I have seen some very strange things in my time, Emma. Once, further north, I came across a race of ape-like people referred to as Heuheua," I said, recalling an old adventure where my dear companion Hans and I faced the worshippers of the monster god, Heu Heu. I did not bother going into details with Emma.

"You see! Apes!" she exclaimed. "Humans and apes share the same ancestry, so there is likely to be links of some sort somewhere. Ape-like men or man-like apes. And you claim to have seen such creatures? Where? When?"

"I am sorry, Emma, but I cannot believe in this theory of evolution. Man is not the result of some random process but of creation."

"Then you are as superstitious as those savages," she snapped suddenly, her eyes flashing with anger. Then just as quickly it was gone, and she smiled warmly. "I'm sorry. Sometime I get a little … passionate."

"My concern now is the slavers," I said, putting her sudden rage out of my mind and trying to alter the subject. "If there really is a species of creature with human and panther characteristics, these slavers may be utilizing them. At the very least, they are disguising some members of their party in order to frighten the locals. Either way, they are going through elaborate means to capture people for their trade."

"But they are only abducting natives," she said.

I paused and looked at her. "Yes," I said slowly.

"No whites, correct?"

"As far as I know, but you could be seen as a threat to their trade."

"Then we should report this to the local authorities."

"I've already spoken to a colonial agent about the matter. Did the officers of the patrol that came here ever mention anything? Of course, they were sent out before I talked to the agent."

She gave me a puzzled look. "What patrol?"

"I was told that soldiers came here in search of me and stayed for a time to make certain you were safe."

Emma shook her head. "We have seen no one but you for months."

Another one of Mortimer's lies.

I waved my hand. "Oh, forget that. I was concerned over your safety when I took ill, and that was all part of my fever. I had dreamt that soldiers were dispatched to protect you and Blake. Never mind."

"But you're certain you saw these panther men?" she asked.

I laughed. "I'm beginning to wonder."

She reached over and patted my hand. "Well, never mind that, now. Stay with us and rest. We'll sort out fantasy from reality. I'm here for you, Allan."

Her hand lingered on mine for a time.

When the door burst open, her hand shot away.

Blake walked in, a glass of whiskey in hand. "Horses all taken care of, Quatermain," he declared. "Took the liberty of having your things taken to the spare room. I do assume you'll be spending the night."

"If it isn't putting anyone out," I said, detecting his negative attitude barely hidden due to his alcoholic intake. This wasn't his first glass.

"Allan will be staying with us for a while, Emerson," Emma said.

"Just the night," I corrected. "I must be on my way in the morning."

"Allan came all this way," Emma said, "to make certain we were all right. He was worried over our safety, Emerson. Allan has had a run-in with slavers plying their trade in the area."

"Really?" Blake asked, glancing at me with sudden interest.

"Yes," Emma said. "It was they who poisoned him and caused his illness to begin with."

"Poison," Blake said thoughtfully. "Yes. I was wondering how you fell sick so quickly, with no other symptoms. Quite unusual, but then tropical diseases aren't my forte. Not much call for that in London, eh?"

"That's not all, Emerson. Allan claims to have seen a panther man."

His took a sip of his whiskey. "Really? Fancy that. Probably a trick of the fever. Makes you think all sorts of weird things. Once had a patient come out of a fever and claim that he was in America the past year and only just got back. Trouble was, he'd never been out of England in his life."

I decided not to argue the point but merely smiled. The whole beast man thing was too incredible as it was, but with my recent illness I could not expect to be taken seriously. Besides, that was really not an issue any more. I had come back to the bush to hunt down the wounded animal so that no one would be in danger of my incompetent shooting. Instead I had stumbled across a greater threat.

"I'll be out of your hair come morning," I said. "I must find Mnqoba."

"That fellow?" Blake said, after taking a deep swallow. "I shouldn't bother. Ran off the moment you took ill. Good riddance, I say."

I suddenly felt the desire to leave immediately.

I stood up. "If you don't mind, I'm a bit tired from the ride. I'd like to retire for the evening."

"But it's still early," Emma insisted. "It isn't even dark yet."

"Well, perhaps a smoke on the veranda, then to bed," I said. "I am still week from my ordeal."

She insisted joining me on the veranda, leaving Blake with his whiskey and his sour mood. We sat in the wicker chairs and enjoyed the vista bathed in the brilliance of the setting sun as I smoked my pipe. She tried to draw me out with discussions of Charles Darwin and Francis Galton, but I refused to be pulled into the defense of my own beliefs. I let her perform a dissertation on the brilliance of these two men and merely nodded and made agreeable replies as though she was convincing me as to their merits. She seemed completely taken by Galton, who had written some work on heredity. I'm afraid that I am no scholar. I have studied the Bible and have read classic and modern literature upon occasion, but I am a hunter and so found heredity and evolution beyond my ability to discuss, especially since I have not read anything by these gentlemen. I did find her mention of Galton's ideas concerning human breeding, in order to get the best traits for future generation, disturbing. Manipulating the breeding of domestic animals is one thing, but interfering with the progeny of people was quite another.

I rose before sunrise. I found it necessary to force myself out of bed, since I had not slept in such a bed since I had left Yorkshire. I have been used to sleeping on the ground or in a wagon over the years, and even my simple bed in Durban was hard and without frills, but I have grown old. Leaving a comfortable bed was a task that would weaken Job's resolve.

Dressed, with my bags packed and in hand, I made my way quietly toward the back of the house. In the kitchen, Jiaying seemed to be waiting for me. She bowed as I entered.

"I make breakfast, sir," she said, and bowed again.

"Thank you," I said. "I'll just see to my horses."

She immediately set some pans on the stove. I could see that the fire was already lit inside. She must rise early each day in order to cook for the hands who took care of the farm and their small herd of cattle.

Outside, I found my two horses tethered to a fence. The saddle and harnesses were draped over the fence.

Josef came toward me from the barn.

"Understood you were leaving early," he said. "Thought I would bring your horses around so you wouldn't have to hunt for them."

I thanked him, wondering if Blake just wanted to make certain I got on my way as soon as possible and had given instructions the night before.

He helped by saddling the one horse while I strapped the pack harness on the other and loaded my bundles of belongings and supplies.

He slapped the neck of the horse. "Good animals," he said. "Be careful out there, Quatermain."

"Always," I said.

Jiaying opened the back door and called to me that breakfast was ready.

I sat down in the kitchen to a plate of steamed buns stuffed with seasoned meat. It was an unusual breakfast for me, used to eating biltong for the past few days. Once the plate was cleared, I thanked Jiaying for the delicious meal, at which she bowed and muttered, "*Xiè xie ni.*"

I slipped out the back and headed for my horses, half way across the yard when the door behind me banged shut.

"Leaving without saying goodbye?"

I turned to meet Emma, standing in a nightgown, arms folded, the frown on her face catching the glow of the sunrise.

"I didn't want to disturb you," I said. I have never been good with good-byes, especially when my own feelings were confused.

I walked back to her.

"You don't have to leave, Allan," she said, losing her angry façade.

"Yes, I do."

"Will you come back?"

"Of course," I said. I did intend to stop by, if only to let her know the fate of Mnqoba or to give her any information I discovered about the slavers.

She grabbed the lapels of my shooting jacket and pulled me close, kissing me hard.

"See that you do," she said, releasing me. She turned and walked back into the house, closing the door more quietly now.

I went to my horses, finding Josef patting the one on the neck. He chuckled.

"She's taken a liking to you, Quatermain. That business with you suddenly ill put fear into her. Never saw her like that before."

"She has some strange ideas, though," I said.

"No stranger than any woman," he said, handing me the reins. "She's a good woman. Lonely, though."

"What about Blake?" I asked.

"Oh, he's sweet on her for sure. Even when her husband was alive. But she won't look at him that way. No, Quatermain, she looks at you that way."

"I'm past that," I said as I climbed into the saddle.

He laughed. "No man's past that."

"What about her husband," I said. "What happened to him?"

Josef just shook his head and walked away. "Terrible tragedy, it was."

Chapter Fourteen

Umgibeli's kraal was filled with activity as I approached. Warriors with assegais and shields poured through the gate and stood their ground in a long line in front of the outer wall, blocking my way. I rode casually forward, knowing this was just a precaution. As I neared, I heard my name murmured among the ranks. Presently, one warrior broke from the others and stepped forward.

"Greetings, Dumisani," I said.

"Greetings, Macumazahn."

I slipped down from my horse but I felt misgivings as Dumisani stared at me.

"I'm looking for Mnqoba," I said.

"We have not seen you for many days. Where is Zakhele?"

"He should have returned a long time ago. And I believed Mnqoba was with him. I fell ill and was sent back to Natal. I've only just returned."

"You were at the Boer kraal?" he asked.

"Yes. And since you hadn't attacked and I was told that Mnqoba and Zakhele left after I took ill, I assumed they came to you and told you about the people at the Boer kraal."

"Zakhele has not returned. We did not attack because we failed to gain support from other kraals. No other chief wished to offer warriors, and thereby weaken their kraals. They were more afraid of rival chiefs. Therefore, we decided to give you more time. We believed you would eventually return to us. If too much time was taken, we would send warriors to watch at a distance. What has happened, Macumazahn?"

"The Boer kraal is owned by an Englishman, but the slave traders passed nearby. They used a dart on me, the same as with your people. I became ill and was sent to Natal. I do not know what happened after I fell unconscious but was told that Mnqoba and Zakhele left the kraal. I thought they would come here immediately."

"They have not," Dumisani said.

"It's unlikely they would pursue the slavers on their own," I said.

"Zakhele would not. He is a brave man, but no warrior. Come inside and join us for the evening meal. Let us discuss what we must do, Macumazahn."

I followed Dumisani into the kraal. My horses were led away by others.

I could not consider a next step. There was no link between Blake and the slavers except for the incident that nearly killed me. We could scour the area and never find any tracks, and it had been more than a week. There was no spoor to follow. When I asked, Dumisani told me that no one had been abducted from the kraal since I had left to visit the Boer kraal, which was good, though again no spoor to find. Since the slavers' trick had been discovered, they would not be able to sneak in during the night. They would expect the kraal to be on their guard for other attacks and therefore not worth their time.

Dumisani had me repeat my story, in greater detail. We sat at a fire in front of his hut. The great hut of the chief was conspicuously dark. The people around me listened as best they could, murmurs repeating the story from one group to the other. Everyone seemed subdued, this whole experience putting everyone on edge.

I was offered a small hut for the night and found I could not sleep, the restlessness of the people being contagious.

When a call of alarm came in the dead of night, I was on my feet with my pistol drawn.

The cattle in the central kraal snorted and stamped from one side of the kraal to the other. Bare feet pounded the dirt as men ran about, and torches sprang to life. Men yelled from different areas of the kraal.

Then someone screamed.

An animal growled and I headed toward the sound.

Chaos sprang out from different parts of the kraal. Shouts and screams and growls. A predator had gotten into the kraal. Someone had left the gate unguarded, which was unusual for the state of anxiety the people were in. Yet somehow a big cat, probably a lion, had wandered in after the cattle for an easy kill.

Sounds of a struggle behind me, with an angry growl and one of the men cursing, and then crying out in agony.

A shape pounced out of the darkness, bowling me over. I scrambled up, pistol ready, but it was gone, firelight catching it as in bounded away. A large panther.

Then to my left something on all fours charged me. It leaped and I fired. The heavy body struck me. I fell under its weight, the wind forced from me. I fired again, fearing its claws would rake me and its fangs would bury themselves into my throat, but the beast lay still on top of me. Struggling for breath, I shoved its heavy body from me. My first shot had killed it.

I could not believe what was happening. Panthers do not hunt in packs. I have seen lionesses hunt together, utilizing strategy, but these were sleek, dark panthers which were rare in this area. I have only ever seen them as solitary hunters. Here were at least two. No, more. I could hear struggles across the kraal.

I ran to the nearest and found one man trying to stab a panther with his assegai. The cat stood on hind legs, batted aside the spear, and raked open the warrior's chest with its claws. By the time I could take a shot, the man had been mauled to death. My bullet hit the cat in the side, dropping it on top of its victim. As I ran in, it struggled to rise and my second shot finished it off.

Further on, I found another man disemboweled, lying next to a big cat impaled by an assegai.

With women screaming, men shouting, and the firelight dancing over dozens of people running in all directions, I felt as though I had fallen into Dante's version of Hell.

I heard a growl, headed for it, and found another poor victim ripped apart.

The turmoil was too confusing. Chaos reigned in all directions.

I tried to concentrate, narrow my senses, drive out all the anguish and suffering, and center on the predators that were the cause. This is what they wanted, fear, confusion, turmoil. I could not be a part of it and successfully hunt them down. I had to remove myself.

Heavy breathing behind me. Not human.

I turned in time to fire.

The cat had just sprung at me, but my shot caught it in mid air. Diving aside, I was able to avoid its claws, though it shredded the sleeve of my shirt. It dropped heavily to the ground near one of the night fires. The light played across its sleek black fur. Slowly it pushed itself over and I readied to put another bullet in it. It looked up at me with its strange oval head. A cat, yet not. It's large eyes glared at me, its nostril flaring, taking in my scent.

It growled, then grunted. The lips of its muzzle pursed, and strange guttural sounds came from its throat. I held my shot, stunned over what I heard.

"*Macumazahn!*"

Things could not get any stranger. The creature spoke. And it spoke my native name.

"*Macumazahn!*" it said again, shouting.

"What are you?" I said.

It took advantage of my surprise and sprang at me, but I am not so easily diverted. I fired, putting a bullet between its eyes.

I heard whispers around me.

"*Macumazahn...*"

The firelight reflected off of short black fur and made several sets of eyes glow in the dark. Four beasts slunk towards me on all fours, in all appearances large predatory cats, with the exception that they whispered my name in breathless, guttural voices.

I raised my revolver and pulled the trigger.

The hammer fell on an empty cartridge, producing a loud click that sealed my fate.

Black metal glittered at my feet, catching the firelight. I shoved the empty pistol into my belt and snatched up the discarded assegai. I was not about to die without a fight.

"What are you? What do you want?" I said. If they could speak, or at least mimic sounds, perhaps they had some form of intelligence.

"*Macumazahn...*" they said. "*Kill...*"

They advanced, moving in as one. The fire was behind me. I had nowhere to go. With a single assegai, it was hopeless.

One cat leaped, and I dove to the side. A second pounced, and I shoved the spear through its chest.

The first beast sailed past me, struggling to turn in mid air but failing to avoid falling into the fire. It screamed as its fur caught alight. It rolled through the pile of burning logs, scattering them. It became frantic, screaming and battling the flames that consumed it.

A third at sprang at me.

*"I heard whispers around me...**Macumazahn**..."*

I happened to see a branch that had only been half way on fire. I snatched it up and shoved it into the cat's face. It howled in agony, batting the branch aside, raking claws along my arm. Blinded, it could not see me swing the branch and bash in its skull.

I turned on the fourth cat, holding the burning branch as I would a rapier.

The beast backed away.

"Why do you want to kill me?" I demanded. "Who are you? Where are you from?"

It growled and backed further from me, its eyes darting between me and the burning end of the branch.

"*Kill ...*" it hissed.

"Why!"

It turned and bounded away.

Around me I heard the cries of the wounded and the terrified. I ran after the cat, but it was gone, which was good, because I was now unarmed and at its mercy. But it seemed to have leaped over the wall of the kraal, and either it was the last of them or any of its companions still alive had fled with it.

As dawn started to paint the eastern sky, I helped find the wounded and bring them in front of the chief's former hut. Some would not live long, their wounds were too severe. Others bore the deep marks of claws that would remain the rest of their lives as scars, but they would live. It was as though the cats had gone on a rampage, attacking swiftly and moving on.

I found Dumisani covered in blood, none of it his own. He carried the body of a young woman, placing her gently on the ground.

"She was alive when I found her," he said, bending over her for a long time.

I had no idea who she was. She might have been a relation, but I could not bring myself to ask him. I wiped away tears with my blood stained hands and turned away, stumbling to help bind a wound and stanch the bleeding of another victim, in hopes that more would not succumb to death before the sun rose higher in the sky.

Hours passed, and no one else died.

What I would have given to have Blake here, to have his medical knowledge and skills to help these poor people. My knowledge of modern medicine was almost nonexistent, yet I could have been an accomplished surgeon as far as Dumisani's people were concerned. Their doctor had been killed by the slavers, and though he was primitive, he would have had knowledge of healing herbs and the dressing of wounds, and natural medicines that would battle pain and infection. What little I carried with me in the way of modern medicines were quickly exhausted.

At mid day I found Dumisani standing over the bodies of the beasts that had caused the deaths and devastation. There were ten of them, some of which I had shot, others that the villagers had killed with assegais. Of Dumisani's people, there were twenty two dead and at least that many wounded to some degree.

In the daylight, they were even more curious. These were not similar to the one that had stolen into the kraal with a blowgun. These were more of the type that had killed Kennedy. They were animals with distorted bodies and faces. Longer limbs, wider hips, longer faces, larger eyes, and shorter muzzles. Their paws were longer than those of a normal cat, though with the same retractable claws. The forepaws gave the distinct impression of stunted hands. They were still cat-like, but so unlike a big cat as to be a separate species. They were beautiful, graceful, and deadly. And they were intelligent.

"What are these things, Macumazahn?" Dumisani asked.

"I don't know. I've never seen the likes until recently. There are some strange creatures in some far away places. Perhaps they came from a place where they have been hidden for ages and something forced them out and into this territory. The way some predators will move when prey becomes scarce."

"But why would they attack us. There is a whole kraal of cattle, yet none of them were touched. They did not come for food. They came to attack us. Why?"

"Did you hear of any of them speaking?" I asked.

He turned and glared at me. "Do not make light of this, Macumazahn. These devils killed many of my friends."

"I'm not, Dumisani. They spoke to me."

He tilted his head, incredulous, unable to understand what I was saying. "Animals do not speak."

I pointed to one of the last ones I had shot, with half its skull missing. "That one did. It called me by name. As did some of the others. And they expressed a distinct desire to kill me."

"Then these are devils, if they spoke to you. They did not do so with anyone else, or I would have heard of it. Perhaps you are the one bewitched and it was all inside your head."

"They aren't devils, or *imbulu*, or *tokoloshe*. They're animals that can mimic men in certain ways. A new species. Nothing supernatural, or we wouldn't be able to kill them."

"Unless they are cursed animals," Dumisani suggested. "We cannot know because our *inyanga* is dead."

"Well," I said, "I was visited by a *sangoma* before I came out here with Mnqoba. She is a daughter to the great wizard Zikali."

Dumisani seemed impressed. "And what did this *sangoma* say, Macumazahn?"

"She is called Izula. She told me there is a great evil out here, but that it is not supernatural. These creatures are not devils. Nor cursed."

"And how are we to fight this great evil?"

"I don't know. She wasn't very helpful in that department."

He frowned. "Typical of witch doctors."

"Speaking of doctors," I said, "I can ride back to the Boer kraal and bring the English doctor back, to help with the wounded. Many are still in danger from their wounds."

"This Englishman would help us?"

"Of course. He's a doctor. English doctors take an oath to help anyone who is sick or injured. Now, he may not have the necessary supplies, but he does have knowledge to help. More than what I have."

"We do not have our own doctor," he said. "If he will come, we will give him as many cattle as he desires. I do not want any more of my people to die, Macumazahn. First we are plagued with slave traders, and now these demon beasts that are neither man nor cat. It is as though the Great-Great has abandoned us."

"Not yet He hasn't," I said. "I'll bring the doctor back as fast as I can."

He glanced over the kraal, at his dead and his wounded people. "If these things come again, I do not know what we shall do."

I didn't know what to tell him. I could stay and watch over the kraal for a few nights, ready with my guns to kill any attacking panther-men, or I could go for help to save some of his people from dying. There was no certainty that the beast men would come back soon. I had seen only one of them survive to run away. Yet there were a couple of his men who would certainly die if not treated properly.

I gathered up my horse and saddled her, leaving the pack horse behind.

Chapter Fifteen

B lake's farm lay before me in the middle of the next day. I had traveled as fast as I could, even during the night, though that had been difficult and dangerous. I started at every sound, worried that the last panther creature that had run away was out there, stalking me as I would hunt down an animal. I felt that I was now the prey and no longer the hunter. I kept my guns loaded and ready, but did not have occasion to use them. Exhausted and with my nerves on edge, I arrived at the lonely farm house.

"Blake," I said, when he and Emma came onto the veranda, "the people of Umgibeli's kraal have been attacked. You must come back with me to give them medical help."

Blake stood silent, puffing on a cigar.

Emma's eyes grew large. "My goodness! What happened?'

I left the horse tied to a post in the front of the house and climbed the steps to the veranda, using my hat to brush dust from my clothes.

"In the middle of the night," I said, "the kraal was attacked. Maybe a dozen of those panther creatures I told you about."

"Oh, come now, Quatermain," Blake said. "Those were a figment of your fevered brain. Did you have a relapse?"

"They are real enough, Blake. Twenty two people are dead."

"You mean natives."

"Yes, of course," I snapped. "Men and women of the Umgibeli kraal. And more will die if you don't come with me and help them."

He blew out a large cloud of cigar smoke and dropped into one of the chairs. "Quatermain, what you're saying is impossible. Creatures like that do not exist. What proof do you have? None. I'm sorry old boy, but you had a relapse of fever and imagined the whole thing. Come inside and I'll pour you a bandy. That should clear your head."

"There's plenty of proof in Umgibeli's kraal," I said, fairly shouting at him. "There's twenty two dead. And ten of those creatures lying dead, too."

Emma's face paled. "How many?" she asked weakly.

She looked about to faint. I took her arm and helped her to one of the other chairs. She leaned on me, her hands gripping my arm.

"Twenty two," I said. "Perhaps more have succumbed to their wounds by now. I pray they haven't, but those who survived need better care than the others have to offer. Ten of those beasts were killed, at least one getting away. No telling how many are out there. They could attack again. I don't know how, but they were able to get into the kraal during the night. They just went on a rampage. If I had thought I needed proof, I would have brought one of the bodies with me. As it is, shouldn't this be proof enough?"

I motioned my hand over my clothes, which were streaked and stained with blood and shredded where claws had raked me.

Emma caught my wrist and turned my arm so that she could see the claw marks caked with dirt and dried blood.

"This must be treated," she said.

"It doesn't matter," I said.

"It will if it becomes infected."

She stood up, unsteady enough that I caught her and supported her with an arm around her waist.

"Will you come back with me, Blake?" I asked as Emma and I went to the front door of the house.

Wreathed in cigar smoke, he shook his head. "I do not practice medicine any more, Quatermain. I am retired. And I certainly will not tramp over the countryside for mythical creatures."

"Then at least give me some supplies so that I can help them. You do have medicines, don't you? Antibiotics? Antiseptics? I'll pay twice what they're worth."

Emma pushed open the door. "Let's get your own wounds cleaned, then we'll discuss it," she said. Before entering, she cast Blake a look that was filled with rage and contempt.

In the kitchen, Jiaying was busy making lunch. Emma had the girl clear a space on the table, placed a bowl on one end and filled it with hot water. She took clean towels from a drawer.

I eased out of my shooting jacket then unbuttoned the sleeve of my shirt.

"I know this whole thing is fanciful," I said, "but I am telling the truth."

"Oh, I believe you, Allan."

"Is there a chance Blake will come and aide the injured people. Can you convince him? He can save lives if we hurry."

She scowled. "He's an obstinate ass. I do not understand his mind, now. He is completely unreasonable. I used to think we were of the same convictions, but this has gone too far."

She soaked a towel in the hot water and proceeded to clean my wounds, mumbling in anger.

Presently, Blake came through the back door carrying some bundles. He dropped a package onto the table, with a smoked bottle lying on top.

"You might need these," he said.

Emma set the bottle aside and tore open the package, pulling out some gauze bandages. She uncorked the bottle and pored some of the liquid over the gouges in my forearm. I gritted my teeth over the sting of the antiseptic.

"What were you thinking?" Emma demanded tightly.

At first, I thought she was asking me, but Blake answered her.

"It's for the best."

She slammed the bottle down, rattling the bowl of now bloody water. She glared at Blake. "All those deaths!"

"Please, Emma, not now."

She leaped to her feet, leaving the bandage only half wrapped over my arm. I began winding it as best I could while she exploded at Blake.

"Not now! That's exactly my point! What has possessed you?"

"I thought it best."

I lowered my sleeve over the fresh bandage and stood up, taking my jacket from the back of the chair.

"Look, Blake. If you don't want to come back with me and help, that is between you and your conscience. At least let me have some supplies like these. I'll buy whatever you have. Even this one bottle of antiseptic could work miracles."

"Keep out of this, Quatermain. In fact, if you hadn't stuck your nose in our business, everything would have been fine."

Emma marched up to him. "You did this because of Allan? You sent them there because you wanted them to kill Allan? Are you insane?"

Sudden heat flushed over me as I pulled on my jacket. I stared at Emma and caught a glare from Blake's eyes.

"Emma! Please," Blake pleaded.

"Allan could have been a great asset to us," she said. "He could see reason, if we explained things to him. Instead you make him an enemy."

"I will not have interference," Blake insisted.

"You're the one who brought it about in the first place. He would have been gone the next day, but you had to foul matters."

"He was snooping around."

"And discovered what?" she said. "Nothing. Now…"

She turned and looked at me with an apologetic look.

"What do you know of these beast men?" I demanded. "Where are they from? Why would they attack the Umgibeli people?"

"I'm so sorry, Allan," she said. "This was not meant to happen. Not now, not so soon. And now so many are dead."

"And more will die if we don't bring some medical help," I insisted.

"It's an utter tragedy," she said. "Ten of them killed."

I could not believe what I was hearing. "You're concerned over the beast men? What do you know of these things?"

"I'm sorry, Allan. If Emerson hadn't overreacted when you first came to visit, you would have left without any problem. But he is an idiot. A jealous moron. He triggered your suspicions. And we had no idea you would be so attached to your man to come all the way back just to look for him."

"What happened to Mnqoba? Where is he?" I reached down to the revolver at my side, ready to threaten for answers, prepared to shoot either of them.

Emma turned on Blake. "Do you see what you have done? I was going to convince him, tell him a little at a time to win him over. But no, you had to be consumed by your jealousy. You were jealous of James, and now you're jealous of Allan."

"But I love you, Emma. I always have. I was just protecting you."

"And how many times must I tell you that I do not love you. I never have. Sometimes I can barely tolerate you. You are a good scientist, but certainly not as brilliant as James was. Don't you think I could get a much more qualified biochemist? You are not indispensable."

"James and I were partners," he said.

"And that is the only reason why you are still here, Emerson."

"I financed half of this endeavor."

"Which is why I am stuck with you, but there are ways of dealing with that. Just do not push me to that extreme. After this stunt today, you are on very thin ice. You may just have ruined everything because of your foolish emotions."

"You think I did that just because of how I feel about you? I've seen how you look at him. You care for this hunter. You talk about convincing him, educating him. You won't be able to. I have seen stubborn people like him before. He'll be an obstacle to us."

"Just let me deal with Allan," she said, waving her hand at him as if dismissing a petulant child.

She turned to me again. "Allan, this is a very complicated situation. What we are doing is for the good of civilized mankind. Come, let me explain it to you. Once we've talked, you'll understand."

"I understand that you, or at least Blake, control these beast men," I said, my mind reeling. "I don't know where they came from or how you found them, but you are using them. And you must have something to do with the slave traders if you know what happened to Mnqoba. Where is he?"

"You see!" Blake said, moving toward us. "He's too obstinate. His mind is one-dimensional. There is only one way to deal with him."

Before I realized what he was doing, he pulled a tube from his pocket and raised it to his lips. I drew my pistol and fired, but the dart struck me in the chest. Blake crumbled to the floor, red soaking his linen jacket.

The kitchen swirled around me as I fell backward, dropping into a fathomless pit of darkness.

CHAPTER SIXTEEN

I awoke with a headache.

I expected to be in my bungalow in Durban, but that was not the case. The room was dark but had a distinctive animal scent. A little bit of light filtered through a small barred opening in a heavy wooden door. The floor was covered in straw and I lay on a thin mattress on the floor opposite the door. It was musty and hot.

I slowly climbed to my feet, head pounding, and peeled off my sweat soaked jacket. Stumbling to the door, I ran my fingers over its rough wooden surface in search of a latch or knob. There were none. Looking through the little opening that served as a window, I saw a similar door opposite and others along a corridor in either direction. The walls were made of cut stones. The air was fetid, with very poor ventilation. What I found most disturbing was that each of the doors had a metal padlock on the outside. I pushed against my door. It was securely locked.

Making my way back to the mattress, I laid down, rolling up my jacket to serve as a pillow.

Words between Emma and Blake played through my mind. They had not been discussing a tragedy against the people of Umgibeli's kraal but of the beast men. Where had these creatures come from? Blake and Emma were obviously able to either domesticate them or control them in some fashion. How else could Blake use them to attack the kraal...all in a feeble attempt to kill me over his unwarranted jealousy. All those people killed and injured, because of me. And Emma was concerned only for the loss of the attackers.

I could not believe that the woman whom I had found intelligent and interesting, and admittedly attractive, had such a cold heart. The loss of her husband and son must have damaged her so deeply that she no longer felt compassion. Yet I had been blinded to the coldness. She had hid it so well from me, though in all honesty we had been together for only a few short times.

Had I killed Blake? I had shot him, as I recalled. I had no intention of killing him but merely to wound him. At the last moment I had recognized the blowgun similar if not the same as that used by the panther-like man who had invaded Umgibeli's kraal. Whatever Blake had used on his dart had been an anesthetic similar to that used in the abductions, so I had little aftereffects. Perhaps the first time, if it had been him, he had either used poison that had made me ill or he had given me something else once I was unconscious which had left me feverish and unconscious for days. He was a physician and Emma referred to him as a biochemist. He would have extensive knowledge of drugs and their effects.

Since Blake used the blowgun, I could only assume that he also had something to do with the murders and abductions. And from their conversation, I could also conclude that Emma was involved in some way. I just could not reconcile either of them to be connected with the slave trade.

Footsteps brought me back to the present. They were the sounds of bare feet quietly stepping on hard packed ground, barely audible except for the fact that there were no other sounds in this prison.

Presently a face appeared in the little barred window, blocking out the light. I could make our the fine black fur and the pointed ears of the small cat-like man who had invaded Umgibeli's kraal and led us on a chase. He apparently stood on his toes to look into my cell, for his head lowered presently and the footsteps receded.

Some time passed before I heard other footsteps. These were different. Shoes on the hard packed dirt of the corridor, not soft sounds of bare feet. Nor were they heavy boots but light and quick.

I clasped my hands behind my head and lay still upon the old mattress. I did not need the flowery scent battling with the moldy stench to know who now stood at the door.

"Allan?" Emma said.

I remained silent, for I broiled with rage. I had been deceived and felt foolish for it. I could not determine if I was more angered by Emma or by my own stupidity.

"I'm sorry it has to be this way, Allan. Emerson insisted you be locked away."

So I had not killed him. What a disappointment.

She continued, "He was in such a state after you shot him. He ordered Josef and his men to put you in here before the drug wore off. I tried to argue, but the men listen to him. They do not think that I have any authority, being a woman. And I had my hands full trying to save Emerson's life. Josef carried Emerson to a room in one of the outbuildings we have set up as a surgery, to deal with emergencies. Well, this certainly was one. You see, I am also a physician, Allan. Oh, I never mentioned it, letting you believe I was just an unschooled widow. It is so easy for anyone to dismiss my intelligence. No one suspects me of being a skilled physician and scientist. I'm only a woman. Well, I'm also a genius. Far more intelligent then Emerson, and even my poor late husband, James. But I needed them, since no one would give a woman any notice, except romantically or sexually. I used my husband's name in correspondence, which is how we came to the project we are now in."

"What does this have to do with murder and abduction?" I demanded.

She laughed, though it was not a pleasant sound. "Oh, those were just a means to an end. Eggs must be broken in order to make breakfast. This is much larger, much more important than you have suspected. The lives of a few savages is a small price to pay."

I leaped to my feet and charged the door.

Emma stepped back, eyes wide, as though I might break through the thick wood panel.

"Small price! All those people taken. An entire kraal at the very least. Are any of them still alive? You are at least responsible for killing the chiefs and doctors of two kraals."

She composed herself and approached the window where I gripped the bars, my fingers turning white under the pressure.

"Doctors? They are ignorant savages. Don't compare their superstitions with medicine."

"Some of those witch doctors spend years learning about healing herbs. Yes, they don't have the advantages of modern technology, but they can sometimes work wonders. Don't discount them because they don't have the same opportunity to learn from universities as you have. In the bush, they may be the only medical help there is."

"Don't equate them with me," she said coldly.

"Why are you even doing this?" I asked. "You kill the leaders to cause confusion. Then you abduct a handful at a time, which causes more chaos because it seems they just disappear. Why? Are you selling them across the border in Transvaal? Or taking them further into the interior?"

"You wouldn't understand."

"Try me," I said.

She chuckled, as a parent might to a child who claimed to know how the universe worked. "Allan … you forget that I have spent time with you. I believe I can judge your intellectual capacity. You are very observant, very logical, but hardly well educated. You had told us you were from England, on a shooting holiday. Fair enough, as far as that went. But I know you were a hunter and trader in these lands since you were young. I know you had very little formal education. Do you think you could contemplate the aspects of heredity? You already demonstrated that you know little of evolution; that you rely on your biblical teachings over science. Well, to me that makes you just as superstitious as these natives."

"Believing in something that cannot be proven," I said, "makes you superstitious as well."

"Nonsense."

"If it isn't too complicated for my brain to understand," I said, "what do you intend to do with me? Kill me?"

"Dear me no. Although I can't say what Emerson wants done. He would probably want to see you dead. I, however, have grown fond of you. Perhaps if you see to reason, we can save you. Otherwise …"

"So you'll keep me a prisoner here."

"If I could trust you, I'd let you stay in the house. Wouldn't you like that? A nice bed? Clean sheets? Dinner served at the table? Could I trust you, Allan?"

"I like it fine here," I said, pulling my hands away from the bars.

"You are so stubborn, Allan Quatermain."

"At least tell me what happened to Mnqoba."

She looked at me for a moment before shaking her head. "No, I don't believe I will."

"Why? What does it matter to you?"

"Oh, it doesn't. The fate of one of these savages doesn't mean anything to me. But it means something to you, and therefore it can be used to my favor."

"Mnqoba never did you harm," I said.

Her eyes flashed and she screamed at me, "They killed my son!"

"Not Mnqoba…"

"They are all the same! They are killers. They are savages. And they will pay!"

With that, she stomped down the corridor.

I sank onto the mattress and contemplated the woman's insanity. She may be brilliant, although so far she had given no indication of what she had accomplished in the scientific world, only made vague claims. She did however demonstrate that her grief had clouded her reason. She was using the beast men for revenge. How had she discovered them in the first place? Somehow, she or her partners had found their land, captured some, and were exploiting them. She and Blake were controlling them in some fashion. I wondered just how intelligent these creatures were. They could speak, but how deep was their understanding?

The small man with the panther characteristics appeared at the door some time later. He rose on his toes to look into the cell, disappeared, then opened a hinged section on the bottom. A metal bowl slid through and the opening was quickly shut and latched.

"Who are you?" I asked. "What is your name?"

"Xiao-ping," he said in a small voice.

"Where are you from?" I asked. "Are you from the land of the beast men?" There was so much I wanted to know. I wondered if he was a hybrid of human and the panther men, or yet another species. Emma had given him a Chinese name, since all her house servants where Chinese, but that gave no indication of his origin.

Nor would he answer me. He left in a hurry.

I found the warm bowl filled with rice, vegetables, and bits of beef. A spoon was stuck in it. I finished the meal in short order, eating every bit, for I was famished. Then I took the spoon and began scraping the stone wall at the door's hinges. After five minutes of labor, the spoon broke, leaving me with a jagged handle and a scoop lost somewhere in the straw strewn floor.

The night brought no relief to the heat in the cell, nor its stuffiness, just darkness. I slept fitfully, my mind creating nightmares from what little bits of knowledge I had of my situation.

It was still dark in the cell when I heard heavy footsteps. Not Emma's light walk or the soft footfalls of Xiao-ping's bare feet. These were boots, and at least two men, one of them carrying a lantern.

The lantern light blazed in the little barred window, then the padlock was opened. The door swung inward on creaking hinges.

"You are a very difficult man to deal with, Mr. Quatermain."

Two men entered, the second holding up the lantern so that they were both in silhouette. I did not need to see faces to know who spoke, for I recognized the voice.

"Mr. Mortimer, how nice of you to pay me a visit."

"I prefer your last place of residence to the present, as I'm sure you do. Perhaps I can rectify that."

"What does the colonial government have to do with this place?" I asked.

"Well … I have been trying to tell you to stay out of this business. It has nothing to do with you. And now because of you, our whole operation is in jeopardy."

"So the government is in charge of this? You know about the beast men?"

"Of course. We funded the research. We helped set Blake and the late Dr. Cairns up at this farm. They purchased it, but we surreptitiously brought in some material to make alterations."

"Like prison cells?" I asked.

"These used to be animal stalls. In essence, they still are."

"So, the beast men are captured and imprisoned here," I said. "And how are they brainwashed to obey commands?"

"It's a rather complicated issue, Quatermain. Something you don't need to know. Rest assured that your government has everything in hand."

"Then my government is responsible for murdered chiefs and witch doctors, as well as over twenty people from Umgibeli's kraal. To say nothing of all the people who were abducted. What has happened to them?"

"I regret the attack on the village," Mortimer said. "Blake acted out of hand and will be reprimanded. Although I understand you shot and wounded him, so maybe he has received his punishment."

"For killing twenty two people!"

"Now, Quatermain, calm down. It isn't as though these people were civilized."

I leaped up and dove toward him, my fist colliding with his jaw and sending him tumbling back into the other man and dropping him to the dirt floor.

I saw now that the second man was Finnegan and he had his revolver drawn.

He took aim at my head.

"No, wait!" Mortimer called out. He struggled to his feet, rubbing his jaw.

"You don't seem to understand, Quatermain," he said, his words slightly slurred. "This is British territory now. The Zulu are a defeated people. Their king is exiled to England. We will not tolerate another uprising."

"This is their land," I insisted.

"Not any more. It belongs to England now. And before us, the Dutch.

Africa hasn't belonged to them for generations. They are uncivilized savages, and we bring them civilization."

"Bringing the modern world to them is one thing," I said, "but subjugating and enslaving them is another."

"Come now, their own people enslaved them. Besides, we have outlawed slavery."

"Then why abduct the people?" I demanded.

"That is something else entirely," he said.

"Where are they? What's become of them?"

"I told you, there are things you don't need to know. If I were you, I'd worry about myself."

"Where is Mnqoba?"

He frowned and shook his head. "Don't worry about others, Quatermain. You have two choices. You may leave here of your own free will and return to your gentleman's life in England, or you can return to England as a prisoner of Her Majesty. Eventually you would be tried, and if you are found guilty of treason, you will be executed. In which case, there is nothing that your friend Sir Henry will be able to do about it. So the choice is yours."

I glared at him, clenching my fists.

"Well?" he asked. "Which is it?"

"I'll go back," I said through clenched teeth. "Willingly."

"Good!" He clapped his hands. "Now you are beginning to see the light, Mr. Quatermain. Mr. Finnegan, you may put your weapon away. I believe Mr. Quatermain will be reasonable from now on."

Finnegan holstered his revolver but glared at me, passing on a nonverbal warning that he could draw it in an instant. I definitely had not won him over. He followed behind me and at ever step I felt his eyes drilling into me.

As we walked along the corridor, flanked by doors to other cells, I kept my head down, hands in pockets, appearing dejected. My right hand clasped the handle of the broken spoon. When Mortimer stopped at the corridor's end to open the door leading away from the cells, I sprang.

Grabbing him by the throat, I spun him around and slammed my back into the door, using him to shield me against Finnegan. Arm around his neck in an awkward position, as he was taller than me, I shoved the jagged tip of the broken spoon into the flesh under his chin.

"If you're going to hang me for treason, you might as well throw murder in, too. Don't move," I said. "Finnegan, carefully drop your revolver and kick it towards me."

He had drawn his gun and had been slow at it, as I knew he would. He was not such an expert with a gun as he pretended to be. However, instead of risking his employer's life on my bluff, he lowered his revolver to the floor and kicked it closer to me. It caught in the hard packed dirt, tumbled over, and lay between us.

I motioned to the nearest cell door. "Now unlock the door."

"What if one of those things are inside," he said, his voice quivering slightly, the first time he showed any fear.

"Then you better hope he's friendly," I said.

He peeked through the barred window and gave a sigh of relief before putting his key into the padlock. He pushed the door open, and I placed my boot squarely on his lower back and shoved him into the empty cell. I pushed Mortimer against the wall to one side, moving the jagged spoon to the base of his neck in order to keep him there, then I was able to pull the door shut, lock it, and pocket the keys. Stepping back, I snatched up Finnegan's revolver and had it aimed before Mortimer turned around, his ashen face staring at me, his hands raised in surrender.

"Listen, Quatermain," he said shakily, "you don't want to make matters worse. At this rate, you won't even make it back to England."

"I don't see how you can make threats when I'm the person holding the gun. Now, where is Mnqoba?"

"I don't know."

I stepped up to him, placing the muzzle of the gun under his chin, where I had recently held the silverware. This weapon made more of an impression.

His eyes bugged out and he turned them back down the corridor.

"Show me," I said, grabbing his shirt front and shoving him in front of me.

"This one," he said, stopping at the third door.

I tossed him the key. "Open it."

His eyes went even wider. "No! You don't understand."

"Everyone keeps saying that. I understand that my friend is in that cell, unless you are lying. I want him released."

"No you don't."

I placed the gun inches from his nose. "Open it!"

He did as he was told, his hands shaking. I heard shuffling from inside the cell.

"Mnqoba! It's me, Quatermain."

When Mortimer swung open the door, a black shape leaped out and crashed into him. There was still not very much light coming into the

"…drop your revolver and kick it towards me."

corridor from the windows in the high ceiling and the flickering lantern. What I saw in the gloom was not Mnqoba. It couldn't be. Yet why would Mortimer open that cell when he knew what was inside. As soon as it attacked the colonial agent, I took aim with Finnegan's pistol, but held my finger on the trigger for a fraction of a second. Then, contrary to my better judgement, I pointed to the ceiling and fired.

It leaped back, allowing Mortimer to drop to the floor, sliding down the wall with a groan. His jacket was shredded, but there was little blood. A few scratches only. He appeared in shock more than anything.

The dark shape stood hunched over and approached me hesitantly.

I leveled the gun at it. "Stay back!"

It did so, cocking its head.

"*Mah ...*"

More sunlight streamed through the high windows, dusty beams filtering down to lighten the long lean body covered with short black fur. And a face with a nose that blended into a muzzle. And the pointed ears that stood high on the head.

"*Macumah ...*"

"Mnqoba?" I said, not believing what I saw.

"Macumazahn!"

He dropped down on all fours and hung his head down.

"What abomination is this?" I demanded. "How did this happen? Mnqoba, what happened to you?"

He looked up, his eyes filled with agony.

Mortimer's moan broke me free of my shock for the moment. I reached down and dragged him to his feet, shoving him into the wall.

"Who did this to him!"

Mortimer cowered under my grip. I repeated my words, shouting into his face.

"Who do you think?" he said weakly. "Blake."

I did not hear the footsteps behind me until it was too late. Mnqoba heard and growled, but remained still. Keeping hold of Mortimer, I turned.

"Blake? Really?" Emma said. "That just shows how misogynistic the government is. Or society in general. I'm a woman, so therefore the man is the one who accomplished everything. I'm just the bloody assistant."

Beside her stood Josef, a revolver in hand, aimed at us. When I turned. I brought my own gun to bear, which left us at a stale mate.

"You did this?" I said.

Mnqoba stood up beside me, a growl vibrating from his throat.

"Of course," Emma said. "Honestly, men are so dense. Don't you see? This is our answer."

"This is an abomination!"

"Please calm down, Allan. Stop being so concerned about these savages and think about your own people for a change. Don't you remember the Battle of Isandlwana? How embarrassing was that defeat?"

"I was there," I said, teeth gritted.

"And my son died there! My son and hundreds more. I will not see that happen again."

"We invaded their territory," I said. Unreasonable demands had been made on Cetewayo. And when he refused to concede to them, the government sent troops over the border.

"We had every right," she insisted.

"It was their country."

"It belongs to us, now. And I will not see others die at the hands of savages again."

"So your answer is to turn people into animals?" I asked, confused.

"My answer is to turn their own people into weapons to use against them. You were in that village. You saw how they fight. Granted, Blake sent them too soon and cost us a great deal in deaths. But still, they wrought better than twice their losses. It is a small beginning."

"It's insane."

She frowned at me. "That is what truly small minds say about any scientific advancement."

Mnqoba started to move forward, but I moved my elbow to touch his chest while I still held aim on Josef. He held back with a glance at me, then made a guttural sound.

"*Kungani?*"

"Why?" I said, translating Mnqoba's question. I doubted Emma could understand Zulu or even recognize his sounds as a word. "Why even do this? Zululand is now British territory. Cetewayo is in exile. Why bother?"

"Because Zululand is in turmoil. Chiefs are arguing among themselves, vying to be the next Zulu king. And when that new king rises up, so will the Zulu people. What happens then? They will attack settlements like this one. They will kill indiscriminately. There will be a second Anglo-Zulu War. And even if that is subdued, there are still the Boers to contend with. We suffered a defeat against them, and Transvaal gained it independence. What happens when they want more land?"

At this, Josef's face flickered with confusion. He turned and stared at the woman with a questioning expression. The barrel of his revolver dropped slightly. Since he stood a little behind her and to one side, she couldn't see the change on his face and ignored his presence altogether.

"So you intend to turn Boers into these creatures," I said, watching Josef's features. He glanced at me, fear in his eyes.

"No," Emma said. "It seems the process does not work on white people. Only on savages. And to a lesser extent upon Asians."

"Xiao-ping," I said. Which explained the different animalistic qualities between the Chinese servant and Mnqoba.

"You've met him, of course. At least twice. Oh, he was an early experiment. True, it's possible that the process was just not perfected. Or there could be some genetic basis for the differences, which is what I believe. We are, or course, altering the genetic make-up of the subject."

"Why do you think it doesn't work on whites?" I asked. The gun in my hand was getting heavy, and I assumed the same was also happening to Josef. Given that and the confusion he was experiencing over Emma's dissertation, I wanted to give him more things to think about other than keeping his aim on me.

"Because my husband was idiot enough to try it on himself," Emma said bitterly, "with devastating results."

So that was how he died or so I assumed that was the result she alluded to. If this process alters the appearance of the victim, and perhaps more, there is no telling what sort of monster he had turned into. All I could infer was that the end process for James Cairns was death.

"What happened?" I asked. "What is this process? Perhaps it just wasn't done properly in your husband's case. Couldn't there be other differences between him and Xiao-ping and the blacks that you've used?"

Her eyes flashed with anger. "Do not attempt to tell me my job, Allan. You are nothing but an uneducated hunter who happened to fall into a fortune. You couldn't possibly understand the complexity of the process. It has taken us two years to develop it. Francis Galton was the first to discover it. Did you know he was an explorer?"

"I've heard of him," I said.

"While he was in the Congo he heard legends about men being turned into animals. He discovered that it was more than a legend, that there was a potion or elixir that could transform a person into a leopard. He only mentioned this form of therianthropy in correspondence with my husband, for fear that he would lose credibility if he even made public what he had witnessed himself. He saw no benefit in it, whereas my husband and I saw it as an opportunity to improve mankind. If it could manipulate the hereditary structure of cells with a sort of de-evolutionary effect, then the manipulation could be used to improve the subject. That was our ultimate goal, to discover how this process worked to turn a man into an animal, so that we could eventually turn a man into something greater, the next step in our evolutionary process. Man into god. But we lacked the funds. We were able to reach the Congo and procure samples, even had some unusual results in animal experiments, but we could go no further. So we contacted people in the government. Some found merit in the project, especially if we could use the results to our advantage. According to legends, a witch doctor can turn a person into a beast, but they become the servant of that witch doctor. Well, we have discovered that as the person changes, they imprint upon the person performing the process. Namely Blake and myself. As ducklings imprint upon their mother after hatching. It is a result of altering the structure of the brain. Your friend there has gone through the process and experienced the same imprinting. Let me demonstrate." She looked directly at Mnqoba and said, "Kill Quatermain."

Mnqoba growled and turned on me, pushing aside my gun and grabbing me by the throat, claws digging into my flesh. I looked into his distorted face, trying to find my friend. His lips pulled back in a snarl, exposing the sharpened teeth. Then his catlike eyes widened. He shoved me back, pushing me into Mortimer, who lost his balance and fell on the floor.

"*Cha!*" he said, turning defiantly toward Emma.

Her eyes widened in surprise. "This is unheard of," she said. "We've never had any problem with any of these beasts before. It's an aberration. He must have a defect. Josef, kill him."

Josef took a moment to register what she was ordering him to do. He lifted his revolver to take aim on Mnqoba.

I fired first.

I regretted killing Josef, yet he had been a willing pawn to Emma and Blake's scheme of kidnapping, murder, and experimentation. He fell over, my bullet through his heart.

Emma realized what had happened and reached down for Josef's gun.

Mnqoba was on her in an instant, backhanding her across the face, sending her tumbling away from Josef's body. He bent down and grabbed her by the throat with one hand and raised the other to deal a deadly strike.

"No, Mnqoba!" I yelled. "Wait. Don't kill her."

He turned his head toward me and snarled.

I placed one hand on his furry shoulder, stopping him, then looked down at Emma. There was no fear in her eyes, only anger, and contempt in the curl of her mouth.

"Go ahead," she said, struggling to speak over the strangling hold on her throat. "Blake will have the others hunt you down before you ever reach Natal."

"Reverse the process on Mnqoba," I said, "and we'll let you live."

She laughed, choking it out. "Impossible. It is a one way process. Eventually your friend will walk on all fours and be indistinguishable from any other panther. He's nothing more than an animal and always was."

I raised my gun and pointed it between her eyes, which now registered fear, for they saw the hatred in my own. I flexed my fingers, trying to squeeze the trigger, but I could not. I could not bring myself to kill someone unarmed, let alone a woman.

"You are a monster," I said quietly.

I looked at Mnqoba, and then back at his former cell. He gave a single nod of understanding and dragged Emma along the ground. She kicked and screamed and beat her firsts at him, until he tossed her into the cell. I picked Mortimer up by the front of his shredded jacket, ripping the material more, and threw him in after her.

"Your heinous project is over," I said. "I will see the governor himself when I get back to Natal. And a few journalists, too, just to make sure you haven't persuaded the higher levels of government with your insanity. Mnqoba will be all the proof they need. And we'll force you to reverse whatever you did to him."

The corridor echoed with her demonic laughter.

I headed for the exit but Mnqoba caught my arm. He pointed to the dozen doors along the corridor.

"Liyana," he said.

"Is she here?" I asked.

He shrugged and began looking into the windows of each cell. I heard an occasional growl from inside various cells.

"We need to leave," I told him. "There are other men here. We have to get away before they know we've escaped."

From inside Mnqoba's former cell, Emma called, "You won't escape!"

"She's not here," he finally said. "We must release the others."

I stopped him before he unlocked one of the cells. "They might be under her influence. We can't risk it. Let's go."

He nodded and we ran out the door and into the barn.

Now more cautious, we approached the doors to the barn. A smaller one opened into the kraal. Opening it a crack, we could see a number of men busying themselves with the cattle, driving them through the gates and out to pasture. There were more men than I thought had been on the farm. All rough looking mercenary types, whether Boer or English. They all carried pistols and rifles.

I held Mnqoba back until the last of the men had driven the cattle out, then we stole from the barn and headed for the horses in a separate kraal. My horse was among them. I found my saddle and another, and proceeded to harness my horse, then found a calm mare to put the second saddle on. Mnqoba hung back until I was done because each time he tried to approach; the horses caught his unusual scent and became agitated. We waited for the last possible moment for him to run up and jump onto the back of the second animal.

Mnqoba's horse took off, spooking all the others, including mine. I had difficulty keeping it reined, while we tore out of the kraal in the company of the other half dozen horses.

The racket we made roused men from the other building. Rifles thundered behind us, spurring the horses to even greater speed.

CHAPTER SEVENTEEN

As we rode, I looked over at Mnqoba trying to control his horse. The animal did not like him on her back. The scent must be strange to her, a combination of man and cat. Mnqoba was a sight in the sunlight, ungainly in a saddle. Black skin covered with short fur. Hands and feet mutilated into paws with extended digits, tipped with claws. A face with a short muzzle and slanted eyes. Pointed ears high on the head. If I had not known it was him, I would swear that it was the same creature I had wounded many days earlier when it had attacked Kennedy.

"I'm so sorry, Mnqoba," I said, though I didn't think he heard me. Perhaps he had, knowing that the hearing of cats is superior to humans. To what extent had he been altered? Would it continue, as Emma had said, or remain at this stage? And could it be reversed?

I recalled the words of the mysterious woman, Izula. *Tell Mnqoba I am sorry*. Is this what she had meant? Impossible. She could not see into the future. No one had that ability, although the old wizard Zikali seemed to do so at times. Izula had also said that a great evil was moving, and that could certainly mean Emma and her project to turn native people into an army of beast men. I had been a fool, deceived by a woman so consumed by the grief over the loss of her son that she would want to wipe out an entire people. Obviously there had been something in her prior to the Battle of Isandlwana that saw other races as inferior. I have met many people like that, who were able to hide their prejudices for a time, but their inner feelings revealed themselves in an expression, a gesture, a word. I had assumed hers were due to her grief. I had no idea that it went deeper, forming a terrible evil in her soul.

"We must go back," Mnqoba said, bringing his horse next to mine in a brief moment when he won control over the animal. "We must save the others."

"The ones in those cells?" I said. "They are all under Emma's control."

"We must try. Liyana is among them."

"She wasn't there. You checked the cells."

"There is another place. Further in the kloof. There is a bend around the cliffs, and another building. Zakhele and I saw it the first night, but never got close to it because of the Boers."

"We can't go back," I said. "We have one gun with four bullets. Blake and Emma have at least a dozen Boers armed with rifles and revolvers, as well as any number of men they have turned into beast men."

"Like me," he said after a moment, looking down at what once had been hands, now with stubby fingers that could barely grip the reins of the horse.

"I'm sorry," I said again, feeling feeble.

"Where do we go?" he said, looking up at me with his pupils now narrow slits in the blight sunlight.

"Umgibeli's kraal," I said. "We need to warn them."

We rode on in silence, Mnqoba once more having difficulty controlling his horse and looking very uncomfortable in the saddle. Fortunately, we were not pursued. At least not yet. Their horses were scattered and it would take time to gather them or bring back the men who had taken the cattle out to graze. They might be able to follow our spoor, although I did not believe they had any accomplished trackers among them, but we had such a head start that it did not matter. They would simply head for the nearest kraal, if not in search of us, then to wipe out any witnesses and destroy the evidence of their abominations. And if they could capture more people for their therianthropy, so much the better in their minds.

When we reached Umgibeli's kraal, two dozen warriors came out in rows with shield and assegai, preventing our advance. When they saw Mnqoba, they all became agitated and suspicious. Spears were raised for attack should the word be given.

From among them, Dumisani approached, ready to thrust his assegai into Mnqoba.

I slipped from my horse and took hold of the bridle of Mnqoba's animal to keep it from spooking, for it was on the edge of hysteria as well as exhaustion.

"Hold, Dumisani," I said, putting myself between the warriors and Mnqoba. "This is my friend, Mnqoba. Lower your assegai."

"No, Macumazahn. This is a demon. They killed my people. It must die!"

"This is Mnqoba. He wasn't among the ones who attacked the kraal. Besides, they were forced to do that."

"Impossible! A man cannot turn into a panther, unless it had been done by the magic of a witch doctor."

"It is true," Mnqoba said, his altered mouth and elongated canines making the words strange yet still discernable. He was improving in his ability to speak, fighting the compulsion to grunt and growl, forcing himself to cling to his humanity.

Men in the ranks gasped and spears were lowered from shear shock.

"It is magic," Mnqoba continued, "from a white witch doctor. Two of them, man and woman. They did this." He waved his paw-like hands over his distorted body. "I am Mnqoba, who supped with you, Dumisani. Who went with Zakhele to the Boer kraal with Macumazahn. They cursed Zakhele and me with potions they put into our blood through tubes. It was a terrible curse, painful. These witch doctors are evil and want to turn black men into animals to kill other black men."

"Why do they attack us?" Dumisani asked.

"The white witch controls them," Mnqoba said.

"And you?" Dumisani asked.

"Macumazahn broke that spell, or I would have killed him. She can no longer control me."

Dumisani turned to me, and many of the other men looked on me with what seemed like reverence, making me very uncomfortable.

"Great Macumazahn," Dumisani said with a wave toward Mnqoba, "can you take away his curse?"

"That is not within my power," I said in all honesty. "Even the white doctors cannot reverse it."

"And this is what has happened to Zakhele and the others who were stolen?"

"I'm afraid so," I said. "At least some. I don't know to what extent they have turned whomever they kidnapped. They are trying to build an army of panther men."

Dumisani's face fell in agony and his eyes glistened in sadness. "Then those who we killed ... they may have been our own people who were abducted. And from Izoqa's kraal?"

"Yes," I said.

He suddenly sat down on the ground, leaning on his spear, shaking his head. "This is an awful curse, a terrible evil."

Mnqoba slipped from his horse and dropped down on all fours. With an effort, he stood up on two legs beside me.

"They will be coming," I said, "to abduct more people and to kill everyone else. Everyone in the kraal must leave."

Dumisani stood his eyes now dark with anger. He slammed his assegai against his shield. "We will not leave. We will fight. Even without our own witch doctor, we are able to kill these demons. If you, Macumazahn, cannot remove the curse that blinds them, then we must fight and kill our own people."

"You can't win," I said. "Besides the beast men, they have Boers armed with guns. Even those men would be enough to kill most of your people. The best way to fight them is to not be here for them to kill."

"We cannot, Macumazahn. We still have wounded who cannot be moved. And we have old women and young children. We cannot have them walk for days to the next kraal for help. No, we make our stand. There are some rifles here, which Umgibeli bought from traders. They are in the chief's hut."

"A couple of rifles are not going to be able to defend your kraal," I insisted.

He shrugged. "Then we will die bravely."

As they conducted us into the kraal, all the people came out to see the sight of Mnqoba. Some were curious, others fearful, and most angry. There were many curses spat at him. Calls for his death came from across the kraal. He stayed close to me, though I could not protect him against the entire kraal if they decided to mob him. I had only four bullets left in my revolver. Half a dozen warriors surrounded us, to discourage any uprising, but that seemed inadequate considering the agitation of the crowd.

At the end of the kraal, in front of the chief's hut, Dumisani raised his shield and assegai and turned so that everyone would see him.

The air fell still. Every murmuring voice became silent.

"Hear me, oh people of Umgibeli. Macumazahn, friend to the Zulu has returned and with him his companion, Mnqoba, whom many will remember. A white witch has cast a spell upon him, as she has upon the other beast men who attacked and killed our people. Not only has this witch turned Zulu into beasts, she has turned them against their own people. Great Macumazahn was able to break the one spell in his friend Mnqoba, but even he cannot break the other and bring Mnqoba back to human form. Macumazahn has warned us that the white witch is sending her people, Boer soldiers, to our kraal, and with them will be other beast men. He has warned us so that we can flee to safety in some distant kraal. I will not go because there are wounded who cannot be moved. If anyone wishes to leave and seek safety, do so now while there is still a chance. Anyone wishing to stay with me, we will defend our kraal and protect the weak and wounded who cannot go."

In silence, the people looked from one to another. Then one warrior lifted his assegai.

"Dumisani!" he cried.

Soon the crowd joined in "Dumisani! Dumisani!"

Dumisani waved them to be quiet, then called to lieutenants and gave them instruction, and the warriors ran to their tasks.

One warrior took Mnqoba and myself into the late chief's hut and showed us a bundle wrapped in heavy cloth. I bent down, pulled back the cloth, and found three Martini-Henry breach loaders. Beside them were two crates of ammunition. They were not in the best of shape, but with a good cleaning, they would be serviceable. The warrior helped me take them outside and ran off to find me materials for cleaning them. I set about breaking them down and examining their workings.

Mnqoba stared at his hands. He flexed his stubby fingers, making the claws extend. "Perhaps these are meant for other things," he said. "It would be difficult to hold a spear, let alone a rifle."

"Then go find two warriors who are good shots with a rifle," I said.

He shook his head. "Nay, Macumazahn. The people still look at me with suspicion. They might even believe I was one of those who killed their loved ones. I had better stay near you."

I agreed with him, having noticed angry glares even after Dumisani's speech.

When the warrior returned with water and oil and old bits of cloth, I had him find two among his people who could shoot. He brought one young man, then helped another to me who had been wounded, with a nasty gash in his leg that had been bandaged as best as possible. Seeing him, I wished I had some of Blake's sutures to help with his wound. But also seeing his anger toward Mnqoba, I decided to sit him down with us so that we could talk while cleaning the weapons. By the time we were done, this man, by the name of Njabulo, and Mnqoba were brothers and he pledged that he would see the white witch pay for the evil she had brought upon the Zulu people.

Dumisani came to me with a dilemma.

"Macumazahn, if these beast men attack again, we must defend ourselves. But if they are men transformed by witchcraft, as in the case of Mnqoba, then we are killing our own people. They may be from our kraal, as with Zakhele. How can I ask my men to kill those who may be friends or relations?"

Mnqoba answered him. "They are under the spell of the white witch, which makes them her weapon. They will not think clearly. Macumazahn was able to break the spell over me, but they may be too deep in her witchcraft to be influenced. It is a difficult thing to kill one's brother, but I would have been grateful to Macumazahn if he had killed me, releasing me from the spell in that way, before I had the opportunity to kill him. It will be the same with the others. We have no desire to kill, but are compelled against our wishes. I for one would not want to live with the knowledge that I killed a friend or loved one because of this witch's command."

Dumisani nodded solemnly. "If we could capture them without putting ourselves in danger, we would. But we may not have time to build traps. And what traps would work? Pits? Nets? They strike swiftly and have the advantage of seeing in the dark."

"Perhaps we can eliminate that advantage," I said, and we discussed some strategies.

Dumisani had sent out scouts to watch the Boer kraal. They never reached the farm, returning at nightfall to say that ten horsemen had already left with a number of the beast men and were heading in the direction of Umgibeli's kraal. The scouts had seen them from a distance, which allowed them time to run back to the kraal with the warning. The horsemen and their beast men would not be far behind.

There were three watch towers along the outer wall of the kraal. I climbed into the one near the gate of the kraal, while Njabulo and the other warrior took the other two. Here we could act as snipers and defend the kraal with the Martini-Henrys. They would do no good on the ground and in the middle of a battle at close quarters. Mnqoba joined me on the tower, which was a flat platform raised above the log wall. We lay down and watched over the starlit hills for signs of the attackers.

Hours passed and my old muscles grew cramped. I twisted to ease the ache in my back, and Mnqoba caught my arm.

"There," he said, pointing a paw to the left.

I saw nothing. Mnqoba's altered eyes, his pupils large to absorb as much light as possible, could detect the movement I was blind to.

"Ten horsemen and ten beast men," he said. "Two are female. I pray that one is not Liyana."

I quietly called down to the warrior at the base of the platform, and he ran to tell Dumisani. Rustling sounds throughout the kraal indicated that everyone was preparing for the attack. Whispered commands passed among the huts. The cattle in the central kraals began to stir, sensing danger.

The horsemen became visible before the beast men, who ran on all fours. The men on horseback waited at a distance, while the beast men ran silently toward the kraal. They were almost at the wall before I could even see them. Before I realize it, three had leaped and clambered over the wall.

"Fire!" I shouted.

I shot one of them before he reached the ground.

My call had not been for Njabulo and the other man armed with the Martini-Henrys. In a moment, piles of wood and brush throughout the kraal were set alight by men who raced out of huts with torches, then ran back to the darkness of the huts. In a moment, the kraal was as bright as daylight and empty of any of its people.

The beast men scaled the wall and ran through the kraal, but the fires robbed them of their advantage of seeing in the dark. In fact, Mnqoba said that it was very difficult for him to see when he looked to the kraal below. The dancing flames mimicked movement of figures, casting shadows everywhere. Furthermore, the scent of burning wood was stronger than that of the people, making it more difficult to locate them. Nor could the creatures find anyone, since everyone was in all the huts facing these flames. When a beast man attempted to enter a hut in search of prey, they were met by an assegai.

Njabulo and the other young warrior took shots at the beast men from their vantage points. Unfortunately, they were not as good with a rifle as I had hoped. One beast man was killed, one wounded, and somehow a cow was shot, though survived to provide a meal the next evening.

I took down another beast man within the kraal, but then we had a new danger.

The horsemen were on the move, utilizing their own rifles. If the fires inside the kraal gave us an advantage to see the beast men and take away their advantage of seeing in the dark, it also provided the horsemen the ability to see us. The towers were plainly visible, as were the men lying upon them.

Several shots tore into the platform I lay upon, splinters flying close to my head.

I told Mnqoba to climb down but to stay hidden, less Njabulo or the other shoot him by mistake. Then I scrambled around and took a shot at the approaching horsemen.

One man flew from his mount. The others scattered, circling the kraal. A horse fell under one of my bullets, it rider trapped under its body for a time and hidden from me. He pulled himself free, taking shots at me but from a poor angle. I took aim on him as he limped away, but was reluctant to shoot him in the back. When he turned after reloading, I fired. He dropped dead, his rifle unfired.

I heard other shots around the kraal.

Njabulo's gun fell silent and I saw him laying motionless on his platform on the far side of the kraal. The other warrior continued to shoot; now aiming outside the kraal. I learned later that his aim became better, as the horsemen were moving slower than the beast men. He was able to kill or wound two of the Boers.

Three horsemen came around and alternated shooting at my position, sending bullets ripping through the logs and buzzing just over my head, forcing me off the platform.

I climbed down awkwardly, carrying my Martini-Henry and a skin bag now half filled with ammunition.

I intended to go to the kraal's gate, where I could push the barrel of my rifle through the gaps between the logs to continue defending the kraal. Mnqoba came out of the shadows, rushing at me. He bowled into me and too late I realized it was not Mnqoba, but one of the other beast men. I held up the rifle with both hands to hold him off, losing the bag of shells. His claws tore deep into the weapon's wooden stock.

He growled and snarled, and when he saw who I was, he spoke in the same guttural way Mnqoba did.

"Macumazahn. Kill Macumazahn."

He ripped the rifle from my hands and stood over me, raising one heavy paw to deliver a blow that would tear through my throat.

And suddenly he was gone.

Another dark shape had driven into him, and now the two shadowy forms rolled over the ground, hissing and snarling.

I scrambled for the rifle and took aim, but I could not distinguish which one was Mnqoba, for surely the attacker, and my savior, had been him, and now the two beast men wrestled each other. Finally they broke apart, but I still could not tell which was which.

"Must kill Macumazahn," the one on the right said, thereby indicating that the one on the left was Mnqoba.

I took aim.

"No, Zakhele," Mnqoba said. "Do not kill Macumazahn."

My finger hesitated on the trigger.

"I must."

"Why?" Mnqoba asked.

Zakhele tilted his head. "I am commanded to."

"By who?"

Zakhele's head tipped to the other direction.

Mnqoba said, "The white witch told you to. She has used her magic on you. You do not have to obey. None of you do. She has cursed us, made us like this. But we do not have to obey her. We have free will, Zakhele. We are not her animals. We are still men inside."

Zakhele sat back on his haunches. "Mnqoba?"

"Yes."

He looked at me.

"Macumazahn?"

I lowered the rifle. "Yes."

"Macumazahn is a friend to the Zulu," he said. He pushed himself up, standing awkwardly on two legs as Mnqoba did. "I am Zulu."

"Yes," Mnqoba said. "We are Zulu."

"The white witch deceived us. Made us … like this." He looked down at what had once been his hands. Then he looked around at the kraal and the dying fires. "My wife? My children?"

"We will find them," I said.

He shook his head violently. "No! They cannot see me. Not like this."

He turned to run away, but Mnqoba caught him. "We will pay vengeance on the witch."

Zakhele nodded. "Kill the white witch."

"Liyana?" Mnqoba said. "Was she with you? Is she here?"

"My finger hesitated on the trigger."

"No. The witch still has other prisoners. She is among them."

I located my bag of ammunition and said, "Stay hidden and I'll see to the Boers outside the kraal."

"No, Macumazahn," Zakhele said. He flexed his digits, extending his claws. "I will see to them."

With that, he leaped to the wall and scaled it on a moment, on the other side before I could even utter a word to dissuade him. Together, Mnqoba and I ran to the gate, undid the beam holding it shut, and pushed it aside. Before it was open, we could hear the screams.

I stepped through the kraal gate, Martini-Henry raised and ready to shoot, and saw only a riderless horse running away. There came two shots, then another horse galloped away, this one with a rider who turned in the saddle to fire a revolver at something behind him. I lifted the rifle to my shoulder, took aim, and squeezed the trigger.

The Boer tumbled to the ground, his horse continuing without him.

Dumisani and other warriors came out, spears ready. They would have impaled Zakhele when he approached, but I held them back, putting myself between them and the poor beast man.

He stood up, his black fur bloodied from other men's blood.

"I am Zakhele," he said. "I am Zulu."

All the others lowered their spears.

Dumisani shook his head. "More work of the white witch."

"The other beast men?" I asked.

"All dead," Dumisani said. "Njabulo was killed by a bullet from the horsemen, but they are all dead too. We lost no one else, thanks to you, Macumazahn."

"There are others at the Boer kraal," Mnqoba said. "Others she turned into beasts like us. Liyana, her sisters, and others. We must save them."

"How?" Dumisani said. "How can we stop this curse? We will have to kill them, or she will send them to us in another attempt to destroy us."

"Will you kill me?" Zakhele asked. "She had blinded me and sent me here to kill, especially Macumazahn. If Mnqoba had not stopped me, I would have killed Macumazahn and then others. Mnqoba undid the spell on me, but not the curse. I am still a beast, but I am still Zulu. If no one else will go, I will return and try to break her spell over the others. Maybe we can find a way to break the curse. Maybe not. We can try the great wizard Zikali, but since this is white magic, he may not be able to do anything. Still, our people need to be rescued from the witch."

"We go together, then," Mnqoba said.

"The woman is one of my people," I said. "It is my responsibility to bring her to justice."

"British's justice?" Dumisani asked bitterly.

"There are others involved in what she and the other doctor are doing," I said. "Government men. I cannot believe they are working with the full blessings of the government, colonial or British. I intend to take this matter to the governor himself, and even higher, if necessary. This is an abomination against man and nature."

"To do so," Mnqoba said, "you must get back to Durban, and maybe England. I do not think she wants you to do so alive."

"We were instructed to kill Macumazahn," Zakhele said, "and anyone else in the kraal, but specifically Macumazahn."

"If we go back immediately," I said to Mnqoba and Zakhele, "I can confront Emma Cairns and Blake, while you find the other prisoners and see if you can break through their conditioning ... the spell that makes them do what she commands. If you get them all away, then I will find a way to take her and Blake back to Natal for trial."

"I will go, also," Dumisani said.

Other warriors nodded and agreed to accompany their captain.

The first rays of the sun were just streaming over the horizon, chasing away the night's gloom. Other villagers braved leaving the huts to find that the battle was over. Some came to the gate to observe what was happening, and murmurs rose up. Whispers passed through the kraal.

After a time, a plump woman came running up.

"Zakhele! Zakhele! Someone said he was here. Is he alive?"

Zakhele shrunk back, stepping behind Mnqoba.

The woman pushed her way through the warriors and looked at each face for an answer. "Where is my husband? Is Zakhele alive? Where is he?"

Mnqoba stepped aside, and her eyes fell upon Zakhele, who looked so fearful that he might run. Yet before he had the opportunity, she pounced upon him and threw her arms around his neck hugging him so hard that his bones cracked.

"Oh, husband, I thought I lost you!"

"Lindiwe," Zakhele said, trying to pull away. "Lindiwe! Look at me! I am not your Zakhele. I have been cursed."

"I know of the curse," she said. "I have seen the other, Macumazahn's friend. I knew you were together, so I feared you too have been cursed. But the curse is to your appearance, not to who you are. You are still Zakhele, still my husband."

"This cannot be," he said, pulling away.

"Zakhele under a curse," she said, "is better than a dead husband. Would you make your wife a widow and children beggars?"

"No," he finally conceded. "But I must go to rescue the others who are cursed."

"And return to us," she said. "Come, your children know of the curse and are not afraid, as long as they know you are still alive."

She grabbed his wrist and pulled him through the gathering crowd.

"We shall rest and eat," Dumisani said, "then we will go to the kraal of the white witch."

Chapter Eighteen

We came to the kloof at night, which had certain disadvantages. However, we had two among us who had the ability to see in the dark. At the crest of the hill that overlooked the farm, we lay in the tall grass and studied the scene. There was no telling how many men still worked the place, but there were at least two patrolling the grounds.

Zakhele talked about the other building along the gorge, behind a sharp turn among the cliffs, and was therefore unseen from our vantage point. It was similar in size to the outbuilding that housed the farm hands and the makeshift surgery. Here other prisoners were housed in cells like those that had been built in the barn, where the old stables had been utilized. Zakhele wasn't certain how many people were there, but at least Liyana, her sisters, and some others from their kraal were imprisoned here. Mnqoba was for charging in immediately, but Dumisani and I agreed not to be hasty.

Even without the panther-like ability to see nocturnally, I was able to make out the two Boers who made the rounds on patrol. I sighted one of them down the barrel of my Martini-Henry, knowing it would be so easy to take down this man with a single shot, even from this distance. But that would alert the whole settlement.

"We sneak in," I said. "Mnqoba and Zakhele will dispatch the two guards quietly. Their vision is better and so are their reflexes. They will continue to the building where the prisoners are held. Dumisani, you and your men will secure the building where the Boer farm hands sleep. If they wake up, you can subdue them. Otherwise, don't disturb them. I will take two of your men to the house and capture Emma Cairns and Blake. If the prisoners cooperate with Mnqoba and Zakhele, they will be led out, join you, and then come to the house. If we have Blake and Emma as hostages, there will be no problem getting away."

"Will you force the witch to reverse the curse?" Dumisani asked.

"I'm not certain how she did it," I said. "I don't know if there is a way to reverse it. But if anyone can do so, it's her, which is one more reason not to kill her."

Dumisani agreed and we moved toward the farm, Mnqoba and Zakhele dropping to all fours to charge lightly over the grass. The rest spread out and moved quietly.

Zakhele came upon the first guard as stealthily as the big cat he had been forced to mimic. In a moment, he dispatched the man with little more than the sound of the body falling.

The cattle and the horses dozing in the kraals suddenly stirred. They caught the scent of our own panther men and became restless.

This alerted the second guard.

He saw shapes in the dark and shot at them.

Immediately lanterns flared on in the bunkhouse. Five men rushed out in various states of undress, carrying rifles.

Mnqoba took down the second guard, but too late now that the alarm had been raised.

Lifting my rifle, I shot one of the Boers. The others fired into the oncoming Zulu, dropping two of Dumisani's men. They scattered. I reloaded and took aim, but the Boers had spread out, taking advantage of the kraal and the excited cattle. Shots were fired at me, for I was now exposed.

I turned and ran to the house in the hopes of entering and avoiding being shot. The two warriors followed behind, but I heard one stumble and fall. Then the next dropped and sprawled in the dirt. With the sounds of gunfire splitting the night, I assumed the worse, but with a quick glance behind me, I could just make out the shaft of a feathered dart extended from the chest of the nearest warrior.

Xiao-ping stepped out of the shadows at the back of the house and slipped a third dart into his blowgun.

I had no idea if the dart held a deadly poison that would kill instantly or an anesthetic that would render its victim unconscious for several hours, a result with which I was all too familiar. I could not take that risk and I felt sorry for what I was forced to do. Without aiming, I pulled the trigger. The little Chinese man who had been turned into part panther fell backward, crashing into the door, shattering glass.

The door burst open and Mortimer stood over the body, revolver in hand. He fired at me, and I dove out of the way. Before I could reload and turn the rifle on him, two heavy bodies came down the steps to crush down on me. I expected claws to rake my flesh, but instead my rifle was pulled away and the revolver in my belt removed. Fists beat against my head. Ropes were knotted around my wrists.

Rough hands dragged me to my feet. Finnegan and Pepper.

Dumisani gave a cry, and Mortimer shot towards him and his warriors. He missed, causing the cattle to panic and press against their fencing. He did succeed in forcing Dumisani into hiding.

"Quick!" Mortimer said. "Bring him inside."

He stepped back as Finnegan and Pepper dragged me over Xiao-ping's body and into the kitchen. Then Mortimer shoved Xiao-ping aside and shut the door.

"Why don't we just kill him?" Finnegan asked.

"Because," Mortimer said slowly, as though to a child, "I don't want him dead. It makes things more complicated. I've been trying to convince Blake and Cairns not to kill him. Besides, if we kill him now, then those warriors outside will storm the house. As it is, they are afraid to attack us because we have Quatermain."

"Oh," Finnegan said.

"Now, take him into the dining room, then help me move this furniture to block the door."

Finnegan tossed me onto the floor of the dining room and shut the door. From the kitchen I heard scraping sounds and thuds, imagining them moving the kitchen table and tipping it over to bar the back door. Other cabinets were moved for reinforcement.

Then arguing voices. Emma's and Blake's and Mortimer's.

My head and sides ached from the beating the two had given me. I struggled to sit up. My vision wasn't blurred and I wasn't dizzy, so I believed they had avoided giving me a concussion, not for lack of trying.

I climbed to my feet and looked around the room.

I had been in here before, as a dinner guest. There were no windows and a single door, which was locked. With my hands bound in front of me, I was able to explore. The one thing dining rooms had were china cabinets, and china cabinets had drawers, which often held silverware. And among silverware one might occasionally find knives. I pulled a few drawers upon and finally located the utensils I sought. I chose one and held it between my palms. Pushing the drawer shut, I sat at the far end of the table, bound hands under the table and out of sight of anyone who might enter. Then I began sawing. It was not a sharp blade, and might even have a rough time against butter, but it was all I had.

When the door swung open, I had not quite finished sawing through the braids. I maneuvered the knife so that it slid into my sleeve and remained hidden, as long as no one looked closely. I kept my hands upon my lap, under the table.

"You have been very bad," Emma said as she burst into the room. "Honestly, Allan, whatever am I to do with you? Emerson tried to kill you. I tried to kill you. You seem very hard to kill."

"You've tried twice, now," I said.

She looked at me in puzzlement.

"You ordered Mnqoba to kill me, but he refused. Broke your spell, as it were. Then you sent all those beast men and the Boers to the kraal just to kill me. Didn't work so well, did it?"

"They aren't back yet," she said. "I wouldn't expect them to be."

"And they won't be back," I said. "They're all dead."

"Don't be ridiculous, Allan. You must have left that village before they arrived, or you would not have survived. Forgive me for acting in such a fashion, but you have become too much of a nuisance. I like you, Allan, and I had such high hopes that I could convince you to help us, to at least support our work, but perhaps Emerson was right after all."

"If I left the kraal before your men attacked it, how do I even know about them?"

She frowned. "Perhaps Mortimer said something. Or you saw the attack from a safe distance. It doesn't matter. If you had been there when they attacked, you wouldn't be here now. It is as simple as that."

"Not quite. As I said, they are all dead."

"All?" she said, unconvinced. "Even my panthers?"

I didn't bother telling her about Zakhele. "Every one. And all of your Boers."

She still did not believe me, but she humored me with a small mischievous smile curving her lips. "And how many of the savages did they kill? If over twenty before, they must have nearly wiped out the village this time."

"I'm sorry to say that one of our men was killed, shot by a Boer. He was a brave man."

"One? One? And everyone I sent is dead? That's impossible! You are obviously lying, Allan. I can't believe anything you say. You've come here to kill me, so why wouldn't you lie. Obviously you weren't even at that village. My creations have probably killed everyone while you were gone. If you actually believe what you are telling me, then you are delusional from guilt, since it was because of you that I sent my men in the first place. But you are not a man to be the victim of fancies. You are a realist. So obviously you are lying. You're just trying to confuse the issue. How would any of those savages be able to survive the beast men attack?"

"We expected you would send them, and we were prepared," I said.

The sarcastic smile vanished, indicating that she lost some of her resolve. "Even if you were prepared, they would still have devastated the village. Why continue to lie?"

"Fine," I said sharply. "Believe what you want. But if I wanted to kill you, I could have done that before, or I could have let Mnqoba do it and have clean hands. Eventually, no one will come back to your farm. Then you will have to send others to find out what happened. But by then all this will be over, and you will be in jail."

"You are the one tied up, Allan."

"Temporarily."

"Don't count on your native friends. We've already taken care of them. We still have some men here, and they were able to chase those Zulus away. And Mnqoba? He fell right into our trap. A literal trap. It was actually created to prevent any of them from escaping. You see, we did have a couple of our experiments get loose some time ago. You shot one of them, remember? Mortimer told me of the incident, with some American dying. That event seems to have sparked your unwanted involvement with us. Regrettable. It took our men days to track the wounded beast down and eventually find the body. Your bullet had shattered the left shoulder, making it impossible for it to hunt. I'm sure it would have starved to death if it hadn't bled out first. The other beast that escaped was eventually caught, but sadly was one of the ones Blake sent to that village."

"What did you do to Mnqoba?" I asked, remembering that she wanted him dead because he broke from her conditioning and disobeyed her. She had no control over him, so therefore he was useless to her.

"He is back in another cell, this one a little more secure than those in the barn. I won't kill him … yet. As long as you cooperate. Honestly, Allan, I don't understand your attachment to this savage. You have lived in Africa most of your life. You above all others should see that we are superior to them. They haven't been able to rise above the stone age."

"They've done very well before we even arrived on this continent," I said, "creating their own empires."

"They are savages," she said, scowling.

"And are able to distinguish themselves when they attend universities."

"Aberrations."

"Why do you hate them so?" I asked. "Just because of what happened to your son?"

"What they did to my son is cause enough," she said with a flash of anger. "We began this work long before. Francis Galton's work on heredity opened my eyes, and I convinced James and Emerson to follow into the field. James had developed a friendship with Galton, but when they corresponded, it was I not James who wrote to Galton, it was I. He thought I was intelligent for a woman, but dismissed me because of my sex rather than my accomplishments. However, he approved of James' marriage to me. He thought our offspring would be genetically superior. He believed in improving the human race through selective breeding and discouraging the breeding of inferiors. I'm afraid I shocked him when I wrote about our own work, based on his Congo discovery. Despite what we do for the government, we will eventually create a superior human being using a similar method."

"You're creating monsters."

"On the contrary, they already were monsters. Or at least animals. We just alter their genetic makeup, give them physical characteristics of other animals. Their behavior changes because their physical nature changes."

"You are changing the brain," I said. "Of course their behavior changes."

"Alterations to the brain are minimal."

"All this to prove … what?"

"You are no scientist, Allan. I cannot expect you to see reason, though I had hoped."

"I don't see any reason here."

"We have perfected the process to alter hereditary characteristics. Change the genetics of animals and people. Soon we can improve our race. James thought he had achieved the ultimate process. It had worked in some animals, but when he tried it to improve his own intellect, there was a problem. For the time being, we use this knowledge practically for creating obedient creatures that will act as our soldiers, so that our people will not have to die in war."

"But they are people!"

She shook her head sadly. "You just don't seem to grasp the simplest concepts."

"How are you even able to accomplish this metamorphosis through this elixir?"

"It is a process. The chemical from the Congo potion involved the use of fetuses."

"What!"

"That is the most difficult compound to obtain, but necessary in preparing the cells for changes. Fortunately, not much is needed for each subject. We expanded upon that, adding in the genetic material of panthers in order to perpetuate the changes in that direction. It could have been easier to use simian material, but we thought feline was more dramatic and could fulfill the military need. Now, the process to improve the subject genetically is more difficult, since we have nothing superior to utilize. We must manipulate rather than combine"

This was horrific. I was sickened, my head spinning at the total disregard for human life. This woman had no compulsions as to what she did, whom she harmed, what lives she destroyed. I had thought that grief at the loss of her son had marked her with hatred, but I could see that she had possessed it long before that.

"I can see that you are upset," she said in a sweet voice, devoid of the monster hiding beneath. "I'll have Jiaying bring you some food. And then you must be sent back to one of those cells. You won't get out this time, I'm afraid."

She went to the door, shaking her head. "Whatever are we going to do with you, Allan?"

I slipped the knife further into my sleeve when Jiaying brought a plate of food, under the watchful eye of Mr. Finnegan and Mr. Pepper. They did not notice the frayed ropes where I had tried to cut through. I might be able to break my bonds now with some effort, but I would have been shot long before I could have accomplished anything.

Eating with my hands bound was a challenge, one that amused my two jailers.

I'm afraid I allowed my pride to fill me with anger and I devised many ways for Finnegan and Pepper to pay for their ridicule.

Blake joined Mortimer to pay me a visit once Jiaying took my empty plate away. The doctor moved slowly and carried his left arm in a sling. I did not know where my bullet had struck him, though I suspected the shoulder, considering his hesitant movements. I did not bother to ask. He was smug, sneering at my predicament. Mortimer was more taciturn.

"I had such high hopes for you, Mr. Quatermain," Mortimer said. "I had certainly hoped that you would have returned to England, leaving me to handle things here. But you had to interfere. Now I will not be able to intercede on your behalf. When I return to Natal, I will try to have you returned to England for imprisonment. As it is, you will not leave Africa a free man, if you leave at all."

"Under what charges?" I asked.

"Treason, of course. You have continually interfered with Her Majesty's government."

"You won't try me for treason," I said. "If the public learns of this project of yours, they would cause a stir the likes of which you have never seen."

"That is why you won't be tried," he said. "None of this will reach the public. You will simply be imprisoned, charged with treason. No need for a trial."

"You can't imprison anyone without a trial," I said.

"Yes, we can. It isn't done very often, and always for national security. The public will know that you have been branded a traitor, and the great Hunter Quatermain's reputation will be ruined. No one will listen to you, least of all Sir Henry."

"I don't want him here," Blake said. "I want him dead. He's bad luck. I don't want him interfering in our work. Thanks to him, we need to replace a number of our subjects. We'll have to start culling that other village nearby."

"Oh, no, not dead," Mortimer insisted. "Dead, he becomes a curiosity. Some fool reporter will start investigating, like that American Stanley who hunted for Livingstone. No, we'll make him secure, take him back to Maritzberg, where I have some friends who will perpetuate the charge of treason. We will discredit him. Let him try to tell anyone. No one will listen and no one will believe him. The whole world will see Hunter Quatermain as a lunatic and a traitor to the crown. Now, if you are concerned about Dr. Cairns' feelings toward Quatermain…"

"I assure you she has no feelings for the man."

"Of course," Mortimer said, not believing him. "As long as she stays focused on the project, now that Mr. Quatermain is taken care of."

"Well," Blake said angrily, "if he causes any more trouble, my people will kill him, whether you like it or not."

With that, he stormed out of the dining room.

"You have become so popular," Mortimer said. He motioned to his two agents, who went to either side of me and lifted me up by my arms.

The ropes on my wrists pulled and I was afraid that they would snap loose. I was not ready for that, especially with two armed brutes dragging me along. But the bonds held, making me wonder if they would break when I needed them to.

Outside, the sun was up and the few hands left on the farm were busy cleaning up after our nighttime aborted attack. One Boer unceremoniously tossed the body of the Zulu who had been shot into a barrow. His treatment of the corpse angered me, but I was in no position to do anything about it. I wondered what had happened to Dumisani and his other men. They had fled under the counter assault, but I could not blame them. We had not been outnumbered but we were outgunned. They would have been slaughtered.

Finnegan and Pepper escorted me past the cattle kraal, leaving Mortimer on the steps of the house, where Xiao-ping had died and his blood still stained the wood.

They took me between the barn and the outbuilding, down the kloof, and around a sharp turn, out of sight of the house. The cliffs became sheer, sparsely vegetated with scrub and vines. The walls of the gorge grew closer, cutting off the early sunlight and making it gloomy. Here was another outbuilding similar to the one used to house the Boer workers. It was windowless, with a peaked roof and a single heavy door at the nearer end.

Finnegan stepped forward and unlocked the door. He swung it outward but did not enter.

"Disengage the trap," Pepper said.

"I know," Finnegan said, irritated. He reached around the door jamb, his hand searching for something on the inside wall.

They were both distracted. If I was to act, I must take advantage of this moment. Afterwards, I would be put into a cell and left powerless. I could not allow my imprisonment and for Emma and Blake to continue their abominations against nature and humanity. I pretended to cough, bending over and pulling at my bonds. The last bit of the rope I had sawn through gave way and my hands were freed.

Pepper was behind me, unable to see the rope coming lose. Finnegan was in front, fiddling with some mechanism inside the dark doorway.

I shoved the unsuspecting Finnegan. He lost his balance and fell into the doorway.

Turning quickly, I slipped the knife from my sleeve and stabbed Pepper's arm as he raised his revolver toward me. The dull blade did not penetrate deeply, merely making a superficial cut mostly deflected by the man's coat sleeve. But the gun was turned, and when it went off, the bullet passed to my left and impacted with the wood siding of the building.

With Pepper caught off guard, I swung my fist, still wrapped around the hilt of the silverware, directly into his surprised face.

He stumbled back, sprawling on the ground, losing his grip on his pistol.

I spun on Finnegan, my ineffective weapon ready, knowing how ridiculous I must look brandishing a dinner utensil. I fully expected Finnegan to shoot me dead, but he was otherwise occupied.

Some mechanism had been triggered by Finnegan stumbling inside the doorway. Springs twang and gears cranked. Something thudded, and in the gloomy interior of the doorway I could see the man's body hunched on the floor, covered by a heavy net with thick webbing. He struggled underneath, trying to bring his gun to bear. He fired, the bullet splintering the open door.

I turned to find Pepper's discarded gun, but found a surprise of my own.

Pepper, blood streaming from a broken nose, had only been stunned and had time to regain his weapon. On his knees, pushing himself up, he raised his revolver to cover me.

My escape attempt went almost as well as the rescue mission.

Then a black shape dropped from nowhere to the space between Pepper and myself. A terrible snarl filled the air and claws raked Pepper. The man tried to cry out as he fell, but could only gurgle through his ravaged throat. He fell to the ground, drying.

Zakhele turned to me, saying, "Macumazahn."

"Your timing is impeccable," I said.

By the time I reached Pepper's side, he was dead, his eyes staring up in surprise. I took the revolver from lifeless fingers.

I turned the pistol on Finnegan and said, "Push your gun through the net, then the keys."

"The others would have heard the gunshots," he said. "They'll be on their way."

"All the more reason you should hurry before I just save myself time and just shoot you."

The revolver caught on the webbing, but was eventually shoved through and dropped onto the plank floor. Next came a ring of keys, clattering beside the gun.

After retrieving the two items from the floor, I dragged Pepper's body through the opening, which led into a hallway with doors on either side. Zakhele followed me inside.

"I thought you were captured," I told him. "What happened? How did you get away?"

"Not I," he said. "Mnqoba. He fell into the trap." He pointed to Finnegan hunched under the weight of the net. Some mechanism caused it to drop from the ceiling when triggered, trapping its victim against the floor. Finnegan had not been given enough time to disengage the trigger mechanism before I pushed him inside. Mnqoba must have been caught in the same fashion, which had actually been designed to stop a prisoner from escaping.

Emma had told me about Mnqoba being captured, caught in this trap, but she hadn't mentioned Zakhele. She hadn't known there was another renegade beast man. Had she known Zakhele had turned against her and joined our ill-fated mission, she might have been more inclined to believe me about her own defeated attack on the kraal.

The corridor was dark, the only light coming through the open door. I could make out the many doors on either side, most looking like the cell doors in the barn. I suspected Zakhele could see better than I could.

"Find the cell with Mnqoba," I told him.

"Why not open all cells," he said.

"Because the other people are still influenced by the white witch," I said.

He grunted and ran down the hall. I looked around and located a lantern with matches and soon had it lit. Only then could I close the door we came through, for there were no windows to let in sunlight.

The first door on left was not a cell door but an ordinary one, striking my curiosity. I opened it, shining the lantern inside. At first glance it resembled a surgery, with cabinets and counters and a flat table in the center. Upon closer examination the table had restraints. Beside it was some kind of pump mechanism that could be cranked and worked like a clock, with narrow tubes running from it. I could only imagine that this had some function in forcing the chemical or chemicals into the body of the victim to turn them from human into an atrocity.

I found Zakhele in the doorway, looking with wide eyes at the room, taking in everything and looking at nothing in particular. He hunched his shoulders and seemed to withdraw into himself, inching away.

"It's all right," I said. "They won't hurt you again."

"This place," he said. "It caused pain." He pinched his eyes shut and stepped back.

"Did you find Mnqoba?" I asked, joining him in the hall and pulling the door shut.

"Yes," he said.

"Show me. We'll release him first, then see about the others."

He pointed to Finnegan. "What about him?"

I wondered if Finnegan had any influence over the beast men, being one of Mortimer's henchmen. I could not take the chance that he could give some command that would trigger some mental conditioning. Also, while we were dealing with the beast men, he might find a way of escaping the net.

"I need to put him somewhere he can't escape," I said, thinking of an empty cell.

Zakhele nodded his head to the room I had just exited. "In there, on the table. He cannot break the straps."

"Will you help me?" I asked, as I did not feel I could handle Finnegan by myself.

Zakhele smiled in reply, showing his sharp canines.

While I held one of the guns on Finnegan, Zakhele worked the netting free. I'm not certain if the Irishman was more afraid of the revolver or Zakhele's claws, but considering the fear in his eyes after his partner was killed, I could guess. He went willing though hesitantly through the door into the room. Zakhele shoved him onto the table and I strapped him down, making certain there was no way he could get loose by himself.

"What are you going to do to me?" he asked his face ashen.

Zakhele bared his teeth and bent down over the man's face. "Experiment!"

Before we left, Zakhele cranked the pump mechanism and turned on its clockwork. It ticked and wheezed loudly. Of course, it was not connected to anything. There were no vials of chemicals, and the tubes did not pierce into Finnegan's veins, but Finnegan was in such a heightened state of panic that he didn't realize this. He pleaded with us, made vain promises, and when the door closed between us, he began screaming.

We hurried and let Mnqoba out of his cell.

"We must release the others," he said.

"That isn't a good idea right now," I said, and made the same argument I had given to Zakhele. "How many are here?" I asked.

"Twenty," Zakhele said. "Maybe more."

"Where are the others?" I asked.

"There are no others," Mnqoba said.

"What? But they abducted almost everyone from Izoqa's kraal. What

"Experiment!"

happened to them all? Surely they must be held either here or somewhere else."

Mnqoba shook his head. "No one else. Everyone else is dead."

I could not believe that so many people would be dead. Ten beast men had died on the first attacked on Umgibeli's kraal, nine on the last attack. With all those they had abducted, how could there only be a little over forty beast men?

Mnqoba indicated one cell. "Liyana is here. Release her."

When I hesitated, he said, "I will talk with her."

"Then do so first," I said.

He went to the door, placing his face to the barred window, and called her name.

She growled, but eventually said, "Who is there?"

"It is I, Mnqoba."

"I remember you. The friend of Macumazahn. What has happened?"

"The white witch has cursed us, turning us into animals. But we cannot change back."

"She is not a witch," Liyana insisted. "I serve her."

"No. She has tricked you. She has cursed you and put a spell over you. She is evil. She murdered your father, the chief. She has used us to kill our own people."

"She killed my father?"

"Yes."

"What about my sisters?"

"They are here, cursed like us."

"Then we must kill her and break this curse."

"I am sorry. The curse cannot be broken."

"Then I will kill her anyway. For my father."

I unlocked the door and Mnqoba pushed it open. She stepped out and looked at us, snarling when she saw me. Then she stopped and tilted her head. "Macumazahn?"

It was a long process, but they spoke to each of the other beast men, several of whom were women, including Liyana's younger sisters. One by one we let them out. On the whole they were taciturn, yet nervous and full of anxiety. I wondered how we were to get everyone away from the farm. There were not many Boers left, but they had many guns. I on the other hand had two revolvers and a limited supply of ammunition.

We made plans to leave the prison building quickly. We had already spent too much time releasing everyone and making certain they were not violent. I was still hesitant and told Mnqoba to watch his fellow beast men closely. It seemed that he concentrated too much on Liyana, their transformations not quashing his admiration for the woman.

I pulled open the door leading outside and immediately pulled back.

A shotgun blast ripped a hole in the thick wood panel, pellets mere inches from me.

"Quickly!" I said. "The back door."

"No," Zakhele said beside me. "There is a door at the other end, but it is bolted from the outside. I examined it after Mnqoba was captured. It is not passable."

I had keys and might be able to unlock it, but if the padlock was on the outside, that would be impossible. It must have been made secure to prevent any more escapes from the building, as the trap of the net had been set for this door. Now our only way out was blocked. It didn't matter how many men they had, one man with any number of weapons could hold us trapped inside.

"Let us attack them, Macumazahn," Mnqoba said.

"To what end?" I asked. "Whoever steps out of that door will be killed. Which one of them will you send out first?"

He hung his head down. "Then we are lost."

"Don't give up hope, my friend," I said, though my own spirits had sunk pretty low and I could see no way out of this.

I heard the crunch of boots on the earth outside, but could see no movement through the hole in the door. For my end, I could also shoot whoever stepped to the door. But for how long? And I did not believe those men were stupid enough to try to enter a building where they might suspect any number of the beast men were free. They had the advantage and needed only wait us out, perhaps taunting us so that I might waste my bullets.

"Allan?" Emma called from just outside.

I refused to answer.

"Tell me you didn't release any of the creatures," she said. "You wouldn't be that foolish."

She sighed heavily when I would not reply. "I'm sorry it has to come to this. Mr. Mortimer would disapprove, but he is not here. We know you killed his two men, and he has fled back to Natal. He didn't want you dead, probably because he didn't want to be associated with your death. That isn't an issue now and I have a free hand, so I'm afraid you must die. Mortimer can deal with the consequences on his end."

I heard her step closer to the door on the left.

"Listen to me!" she shouted suddenly. "I command you, kill Allan Quatermain!"

Behind me, a dozen beast men stirred. They growled and snarled. They shuffled toward me in a single mass.

I had only a few bullets in each of the two revolvers. I might find more ammunition on Pepper's body, which lay beside me, but I doubted I would be given the opportunity to reload before I was overwhelmed. I saw that Pepper had a sheathed knife attached to his belt, and I could grab that to help even the odds when my bullets were exhausted. It was not much, but it was the only chance I had.

Turning, I prepared to sell my life dearly. I loathed to kill these creatures now, for they were innocent victims of Emma's twisted scheme. They were her creation, her puppets. Perhaps if I burst through the door and killed her, her influence over them would be terminated. Yet I would no doubt be shot by her Boers before I stepped outside. Furthermore, I could not escape my own Victorian mores and balked at the idea of killing a woman, armed or not, no matter how evil she might be. Obviously I would if I had to, if it was the only way to preserve my own life, but I would make that involuntary hesitation which would be my downfall.

Mnqoba and Zakhele stood between me and the other transformed people. Liyana was in the lead, glaring at me with hatred.

"No!" Mnqoba said, grabbing hold of the woman and shaking her violently. "Macumazahn is not your enemy. He is our friend. The white witch is the enemy. She did this to us. Do not listen to her."

"The white witch?" one of the others said.

"Do not listen to her!" Zakhele said.

"Kill the white witch!" another said.

"No! Don't do that," I shouted back. "If you kill her, you lose any chance of turning back into humans. She did this to you, she is the only one who can reverse it."

"Kill the witch!" others yelled,

Our exchange had been in Zulu, which Emma would not understand. She had no idea that she had so easily lost control of her creations and that she was now in danger.

As a mob, they overwhelmed Zakhele and Mnqoba as they would have if they were to follow Emma's commands to kill me. Mnqoba tried to hold Liyana back, but he was overpowered by the others. They swept me aside and pushed through the door.

I heard the first gunshot and feared the worst, that they would be slaughtered, but no more shots came.

Instead, I heard other shouts. It was a cry I had not heard since that terrible day of the battle of Isandlwana.

"*Usuthu!*"

I scrambled to my feet and ran outside. The scene so surprised me that I stopped dead and stared. On one side were the beast men, on the other were Zulu warriors led by Dumisani. Between them were the few Boers who had remained, all dead, at least two still with spears sticking out of their bodies. One of the panther men lay dead, shot as he had been the first to exit the building. Now the Zulu faced those who had once been their own people. Out of fear they would spear the beast men, knowing what others had done in their own kraal. Out of similar fear, the transformed humans would attack. Who would survive?

"Wait!" I shouted, running through to place myself between the two forces. "Put down your assegais. Do not attack! These are your people. Do not be afraid!"

I waved my hands from one group to another.

Zakhele stepped out. "These are my brothers," he said to his fellow beast men, motioning to the warriors. "Do not harm them." Then he turned to Dumisani and pointed to the panther creatures at his back. "These are my brothers, do not harm them."

The warriors lowered their assegais and the beast men bowed their heads in a sign of submission.

Among the panthers, Liyana stood with both her paws-like hands around the neck of Emma.

I ran to them, with Mnqoba coming up on the other side.

"Don't kill her," I said, trying to remain calm so as to not excite either woman.

"The witch must die," Liyana hissed. "She killed my father. She did *this* to me, to my sisters."

"And she is the only one who has the power to reverse it," I said. "The only one with the knowledge."

"Then make her do so," Liyana said, without releasing her grip.

Emma's face was purple, her mouth gaping, gasping for breath through a constricted throat. Her eyes were wide with fear.

"Emma," I said, and her eyes turned from the panther woman to me. "Tell them you will do what you can to change them back. Promise them."

She gave a short, gurgling laugh. "Why would I do that?" she asked.

"It is the only way to save your life," I told her. "Change them back to human."

"Dear Allan, this isn't magic. This is science. Certainly the process may be reversible, but do you realize what it entails? I would need to create new chemicals based on human heredity rather than panther. If I used panther and human fetal material before, I would need to use at least twice as much human fetal material for the reversal, if it would even work. Do you realize how many pregnant woman we would need?"

Liyana looked at me, her angry slit eyes flashing, waiting for me to translate.

I did so.

Liyana ripped out Emma's throat and dropped her dying body onto the dirt. Emma gasped and struggled, her hands grasping at her ruined, gaping neck until she died, her eyes staring up at the cloudless sky.

CHAPTER NINETEEN

I looked over the scene of death. Emma and her Boer mercenaries, Mortimer's man Pepper. I remembered Finnegan strapped down in the surgery. I couldn't allow the beast people or Dumisani's warriors to kill him, too.

"Inside the building is an Irishman," I said. "He is my prisoner, to be taken back to Natal. No harm is to come to him."

Dumisani nodded. The others either grunted or remained silent.

"Is everyone else dead?" I asked Dumisani.

"Everyone out here," he said. "There is no one in the barn or other building. I do not know about the house. The woman came alone from the house. I saw one skinny white man leave on horseback, but that is all."

I had him follow me into the former prison where we entered the room and found Finnegan still strapped to the table.

He screamed when we pushed open the door, his eyes wide with terror.

"Don't touch me! Leave me alone! I didn't do anything to any of you."

He threw his head back and forth, wiggling against the bonds.

"Easy, man," I said. "No one is going to hurt you."

"*They* are! They are going to put that stuff through my veins and turn me into some sort of animal."

"Who?" I asked.

"Blake and Cairns. And Mortimer. Especially Mortimer. He's behind the whole thing, turning people into animals, making an army of beast people."

"Dr. Cairns is dead," I said. "Mortimer ran away. We'll find Blake and see that he pays for what he has done. No one else will do any more experiments."

"Are you sure, Quatermain? Please, I'll do anything, just get me out of here."

I patted his shoulder reassuringly. "I'll take you back to Natal myself, as long as you go with me to the governor and testify against Mortimer and the others."

"Anything!" he said with a glimmer of hopefulness. "Just get me out of here."

"You are my prisoner, so we will tie your hands, but no one will harm you. You have my word."

He nodded enthusiastically.

I undid the straps and Dumisani brought some bits of rope to bind his wrists, then two warriors escorted him out, more for his protection from the beast men than to keep him secured.

Dumisani and I led the way to the house, followed by his warriors, with the beast men slinking behind. Mnqoba held back with what I can only describe as his people. Liyana and Zakhele were on either side of him. The other beast men and women seemed to be drawn to Mnqoba for guidance. They had all been under Emma Cairns' control for so long that they were uncertain how to act now that they were free. Mnqoba showed them that they could fight the animal instincts that were so dominant after their transformation, and each of them was trying to mimic Mnqoba in walking upright, though some fell upon all fours from time to time.

I went into the kitchen, brandishing my two revolvers, and found Jiaying cowered under the heavy table.

I bent down and looked into her frightened face. "Do you understand me?" I asked.

She nodded vigorously, staring wide-eyed at the revolvers.

"I won't hurt you," I said.

"Xiao-ping dead?" she asked.

"Yes," I said. "And so is Dr. Cairns. Where is Dr. Blake? And Kuan-yin, where is he?"

"Front room," she said. "Xiao-ping was husband."

"I'm sorry," I said.

"She turn him, made him beast. Made him obey her. Gave him poison darts to use. Not his fault."

"I know. You can leave, now. No one will hurt you. You are free to go."

"Where?" she said, bursting into tears, folding up into a tiny ball under the table. "Go where?"

I stood up, not knowing what to say.

Dumisani and half of his warriors followed me into the front room of the house. We found Blake in a thickly padded chair, a glass of whiskey in his hand. His head leaned back, his bleary eyes looking around as though they did not see the walls of the house. Kuan-yin stood at his side, holding a silver tray with a crystal decanter. He inclined his head toward me in greeting, as though I often dropped by with half a dozen Zulu warriors to accompany me.

I lowered my revolvers, seeing no threat from Blake.

He turned his head as we entered, his blood-shot eyes taking time to focus.

"Ah, Quatermain. 'Bout time. Suppose everything has fallen apart, eh? I tried to warn Emma, but she was rather taken by you. Can't understand why? She's always been a difficult woman to understand. Her husband was completely devoted to her. Brilliant man, James was. But even he could not hold a candle to Emma. She had such high hopes for their son, coming from such intellectual stock, you know, improving mankind by better breeding. Then he joined the bloody army. Nearly devastated Emma. She completely lost it when he was killed. Where is she, by the way? We heard shots some time ago and she decided to take the remaining men and put an end to you. Apparently she was not successful."

"She's dead," I said evenly.

"Pity. I told her how I felt about her after James died, but she just laughed it off. Idiot of a husband was so blinded by her, he tried their own experiments. Too early in the process. Animal trials had gone well, but it was too soon for human experimentation. Actually, it was Emma who said he decided to test in on himself. I really suspected that she did it without his consent, trying to make him more intelligent. What resulted was not a pretty picture, nor did it live long. So, Quatermain, did you shoot her?"

"No. She was killed by one of her creations. Chief Umgibeli's daughter, Liyana."

"Probably a tad upset about her father. Understandable."

"You'll come back with me," I said. "You'll have to testify on what Emma did."

"'Fraid not, old boy," he said, taking a healthy swallow of his whiskey.

He held the glass up, looking into the light glistening through the liquid. "You see, I put the same poison we used on the old chief in my glass. Had tried to work up my courage to take it, and now that I know Emma is gone, then I can make an end to everything. Damn you, Quatermain, for coming here."

"Mortimer is still out there," I said. "This isn't over."

But for Emerson Blake, it was.

We left Kuan-yin to deal with the disposition of the body, or rather all the bodies. I told him to take care of Jiaying, to which he nodded and replied that she was his sister. He had no desire to stay, and soon left the farm with Jiaying in a wagon from the barn, now filled with belongings, probably valuables pilfered from their former employer. They could not be begrudged since Jiaying lost her husband because of them in two ways. First, he was changed by their experiments, and then killed when he tried to obey his mistress and shoot me with one of his darts. I felt a pang of guilt for having killed him, but I had no choice.

Dumisani had his warriors take whatever weapons they could find, then released all the goats and cattle to drive them back to their kraal. As compensation, Dumisani said.

"What about Zakhele and the others?" I asked Dumisani as he stayed behind for a few moments.

He shook his head. "They cannot come to our kraal, Macumazahn."

Zakhele heard this and immediately became exited. "But my family! My wife and children are there. I cannot leave them."

"You cannot exile them," I told Dumisani. "Some of them come from your kraal, like Zakhele and Liyana. Liyana and her sisters are the chief's daughters."

"And many of our people were killed by the beast men," he insisted. "What of their families, who would be reminded of this each time they see one of them."

"So you would even drive away Umgibeli's daughters?" I demanded sharply.

Liyana and Mnqoba came to us, having overheard our conversation, which was becoming heated. She placed a paw on my arm and looked at me with greenish slit eyes.

"Dumisani is right, Macumazahn. We cannot go back to the kraal. We have discussed it among ourselves."

All the other beast people circled us.

"We will start our own tribe," Mnqoba said.

"And your father's people?" I asked Liyana.

"They have Dumisani," she said. "He is a good leader. Besides, who would marry me now? I am no longer the desirable princess you first saw."

"I disagree," Mnqoba said, putting his arm around her shoulders.

She smiled at him, then turned back to me. "Mnqoba is now my chief. Together we will start a new tribe, far away from here."

"Perhaps the jungles to the west," Mnqoba said. "There will be plenty of prey for panthers and very few people to bother us. Perhaps we will stay like this the rest of our lives, perhaps we will turn completely into panthers, though I doubt it since we have not changed at all since the first time. We are panther men, and there will be legends spoken of us."

He laughed and the others joined in. Except for Zakhele, who hung his head down and hunched over so that he was almost on all fours.

Dumisani looked at him for a long time before he spoke. "Zakhele. You have fought well today. If not for you, Macumazahn would have been imprisoned and the day would have been much different. Let us honor you by inviting you to return with us."

Zakhele's eyes widened and his mouth dropped open. "Return?"

"Yes. I suppose just one of you would not cause our people's hearts to ache too much. If your wife can accept you as this, so can we. You are brave and honorable, and this was not your fault."

Zakhele bowed, trembling with joy. "Thank you, Chief Dumisani."

Dumisani motioned him along, and they both followed the warriors driving the cattle across the veldt.

While Mnqoba and the others made preparations, I saddled two horses and loaded a third with supplies. I brought Finnegan, with his wrists still bound, and helped him onto one of the horses. The man was pale and very subdued; a shadow of his former braggart shelf. He sat meekly in the saddle, avoiding eye contact.

"Watch that one, Macumazahn," Mnqoba said.

"I will," I said. "I'm so sorry, Mnqoba." Then I remembered what Izula had told me before she had left my house. Had she known what would happen to him? No. That had merely been a trick; something like Zikali would do to me to make me believe in supernatural powers. She probably believed that Mnqoba would be captured by slavers or killed or some other tragedy befall him. Or if nothing happened, I would not have even recalled those parting words. Just a trick.

"No need, Macumazahn. I have the princess I desired, even paid for by the cattle from this kraal that Dumisani took with him. Now I will be a chief. A small tribe, but a very unique tribe. I was a wanderer, with no direction, no purpose, no one to share my life. Now I have all of those. But there is one whom I wish to tell, so that she does not worry about me. My cousin, who is with child. Could you find her and tell her that I am well. If you say that I am now a chief, married to a chief's daughter, she might be proud of me."

I took him and embraced him. "She would be very proud indeed. As am I, Mnqoba. If you ever need me…"

"Nay, Macumazahn, for you will go back to England, I think, to your own family. But perhaps you will think of Mnqoba once in a while. Mnqoba, chief of the beast men."

CHAPTER TWENTY

We headed for Maritzburg.

If Mortimer was to save himself, he might go there before Durban. Finnegan and I were a sight, covered in dust from travelling, clothes torn and filthy from our adventures and struggle. When we approached the colonial government building, we were immediately stopped by a colonial captain. He eyed us with confusion and suspicion, especially Finnegan, still with his hands tied in front of him.

"I am Allan Quatermain," I said, exhausted. "I need to speak with the governor."

"Oh, of course, I'm sure Sir Henry is expecting you," he said, sarcastically referring to Governor Bulwer.

"No," I said, "but Sir Henry Curtis is probably awaiting my return to Yorkshire. Could you please send a message to the governor?"

The captain stopped smirking. "Sir Henry Curtis? I've heard that name before. Wait, what did you say your name was? Quatermain? Not Hunter Quatermain! Why, you discovered King Solomon's mines. What are you doing here?"

"Trying to see the governor. It's rather urgent."

This captain passed me to a British colonel, who also looked me over with a similar distaste that the captain had experienced originally.

"Quatermain?" he said. "Isn't that the chap we're supposed to arrest? The one from Durban."

"Must be another Quatermain," the captain said. "This is Hunter Quatermain. You know, King Solomon."

"Oh, that business with the lost mines. No, I still think we're supposed to arrest him."

"If I could just speak with the governor," I said.

"Look, Mr. Quatermain, we don't let just anyone in to see Sir Henry Bulwer. Especially in your state."

"Just give him my name. Mention Sir Henry Curtis, if you like. Mention Cetewayo, too, if it will do any good."

He shrugged, left me in an empty office with Finnegan, and eventually returned in a more taciturn mood.

"His lordship will see you now," he said, somewhat chastised.

I had never met the governor before, but he was pleased to make my acquaintance, pumping my hand as Finnegan, now free of his bonds, and I were escorted into his office. We sat in large chairs in front of a massive desk. Governor Bulwer beamed at me.

"I have heard so much about you, Mr. Quatermain. We have a number of mutual friends, from many different social circles. It seems you have quite a reputation. This recent business that has come to my attention does not ring true, something about murders. I granted you this interview because of your public standing and my own curiosity, rather than allowing for your arrest and trial. Do you mind answering these charges?"

"I have come today to offer my own charges against Elliot Mortimer," I said.

"Indeed? And what are those?"

"Treason, for one. Perhaps I should start at the beginning, if you have time."

"By all means. You have my full attention."

For an hour we sat, while I told my story. He was enraptured, interrupting me upon occasion with a question or two for clarification, and once to call for tea. Eventually, when I was done and exhausted, he looked at Finnegan.

"And you are this Mr. Finnegan?" the governor asked.

Finnegan grew very stiff and alert. "Aye, m'lord. Sean Finnegan, Sergeant Major, formerly of the Eleventh Bengal Lancers."

"And how were you discharged from Probyn's Horse, Sergeant Major?"

"Wounded in Afghan, m'lord."

"So you and this other man had been hired by Mortimer. Highly unorthodox. Can you corroborate any of what Mr. Quatermain has told me?"

"M'lord, I wasn't present for it all, but what I gather, every word in God's truth."

"Mr. Quatermain," the governor began after a moment of thoughtfulness, "these are very serious charges you make against one of our colonial agents, as well as against these deceased scientists. Such an incredible story that I wished you were able to bring one of these people to me, in which case any doubt as to your veracity would vanish. However, I would not want to subject any of those poor devils to any more unease. Nor would I want to subject Her Majesty's government to the embarrassment of explaining how her citizens and representatives perpetrated these atrocities. It is best, as you have said, that they have made their way into isolation. I will personally send investigators to these tribes and if we find what you say is true, of which I have no doubt, we will send aid to these people. Furthermore, I will interview Mr. Mortimer to determine the extent of his involvement. I assure you that he has acted without my knowledge and I will discover with who in the government he was in league."

"And will you require our testimonies, m'lord?" I asked.

"I very much doubt it, Mr. Quatermain. I understand that you will want to return to England as soon as you are able. Mr. Finnegan will no doubt be available to us, if necessary. I would rather not have this situation dragged into the courts and therefore on display in front of the public. We have suffered enough embarrassments of late; we do not need any more. We will investigate this farm Blake and Cairns owned, take away any records that they might have left, so that this is never repeated. This incident will disappear as though it never happened, though I am sorry for the many victims it has left."

"And Mortimer?" I asked,

A small smile played over the governor's face. "I'm certain he will make a full confession to me, Mr. Quatermain, and I assure you that he will be reassigned to a place where he will never have an opportunity to abuse his power again. A very distant and uncomfortable place."

Therefore, filled with Governor Bulwer's promises, and after making my own promise that I would not repeat this story for some time to come, we bade him farewell.

Finnegan seemed to come alive when we returned to our horses. He was no longer the dejected, fearful man who had left with me, nor was he the rough, arrogant character who had bullied me and made me prisoner several times. He was a new creation and very grateful for his new lease on life, as he said. He had expected to be thrown into prison for his involvement in recent events and was ecstatic to be free.

"Mr. Quatermain, Squire, sir, I can't thank you enough. Saints be praised, you are my savior, sir. I promise, the man you knew is dead, buried back there with poor Pepper. You, sir, have taught me humility. I will not disappoint you, Squire."

"What will you do now, Finnegan?" I asked as we rode on to Durban.

"Don't know, but I will no longer serve as a mercenary. I have seen enough killing; I don't want any more hand in it. Perhaps I'll try my hand at trading, as you did."

And as we rode, he asked me of my trading experiences, while I marveled at the change in him.

In Durban we said our good-byes. He asked if he might correspond with me, and I insisted upon it. I had found this newly transformed Irishman an enjoyable companion and was curious how he would do with his new outlook on life. I went as far as to withdraw funds through my Durban bank in order to finance his first trading expedition, although I had in mind merely to keep him from falling into his old life if he became too low on money. He was very happy with the fact that he was now partners with Hunter Quatermain.

Some days later, I packed up what remained in my little bungalow and prepared myself for leaving Africa for what I believed would be the last time.

When I turned around, the shapely form of a woman stood silhouetted in my doorway, startling me as I had not heard her enter.

"That was very touching," Izula said.

"Don't you ever knock?" I asked.

"Your door was open."

"No, it wasn't. What do you want?"

"I said, that was very touching."

"Yes, I heard you. What do you mean?"

"What you did for Mnqoba's cousin, Sizani."

"Do you follow me around?" I asked.

"No. But I hear many things. The spirits tell me much. Oh, you do not believe in the spirits."

"I believe in the one."

"Of course. The Spirit of the Great-Great. He is the Spirit over all others, but there are many minor spirits, and from them I learned of your visit to Sizani and her husband Khulekani. You told them about Mnqoba, but not what happened to him, not his transformation."

"How did you know about that?"

I had gone to their little home on the outskirts of Durban to tell Sizani about the bravery of her cousin, and that he had married the beautiful daughter of a chief, and that he had become a chief himself. If he would ever come back to Natal, it would not be for a very long time, for now he had the great responsibilities of being a good husband and leader to his people. Sizani was very impressed, wiping tears from her eyes when I told her about his bravery in saving these people and becoming their chief. Never did I mention the beast men, or that Mnqoba was one of them, transformed into a panther man by a twisted genius. There was no need for her to know. And there was no way Izula could know.

"You do not believe me when I tell you. Why did you give them your house? That was not necessary," she said.

"None of your business," I said, irritated. Her knowing that made more sense, since she could have overheard Sizani and her husband telling others that they would be moving. Before I had visited them, I paid a visit to my solicitor. I made arrangements that they would live in my house rent-free as caretakers for as long as they cared. If any repairs needed to be made, my solicitor would see to it, drawing funds from my Durban bank. A small stipend would also be paid each month to Khulekani in his capacity as caretaker. In the event of my death, the house would be deeded to them. Khulekani was a proud man and would not accept the offer. I had explained that I needed someone to live in the house and take care of it, as it held too many memories and I did not want to sell it. Furthermore, I was honoring my friend Mnqoba in doing so and paying a debt I owed to Khulekani for his help previously on the steamship, *Song of Solomon*. I assured them that they would be doing me more of a favor than I was doing them, and Khulekani finally agreed. I could see a great weight lift from him and he was very happy, though would not show it.

"Did you," Izula said, "tell Mnqoba that I was sorry."

"You did not come up in conversation."

A smile played across her shapely lips. "He is a good man and will be a good chief."

"I have no doubt," I said.

"You will miss him as you miss others, many of them who have gone over," she said, using the euphemism for death.

This gave me pause, and images flashed through my mind. Hans, Maria, Stella, my father, even Mameena. So many. My age weighed heavy on me.

"But," she said brightly, "you will not be leaving so soon."

"I have a cabin booked on a steamship. Everything is taken care of. I am done with Africa and going home to Yorkshire."

"Africa is your home, and she is not done with you yet. The spirits …
oh, I am sorry. You only believe in the one. Well, seek out the Spirit of the
Great-Great, and He will tell you. You are needed, Macumazahn, Watcher-
by-Night, the great Hunter Quatermain."

"Needed? For what?"

"Only you can defeat the *impundulu*, the lightening bird. You must
come with me now, before others die. And on the way, we will find your
friend, the Irishman, Finnegan. You will need his help."

END

ABOUT OUR CREATORS

AUTHOR –

Wayne Carey—A life-long fan of science fiction and pulp fiction, Wayne Carey grew up reading Edgar Rice Burroughs, H.G. Wells, Isaac Asimov, H. Rider Haggard and all the grand masters, which guided him toward a career in science with degrees in biology and education and provided the desire to write from an early age. A love of classic and noire films, such as *Casablanca* and *The Maltese Falcon*, also influences his writing. He is the author of *The Nanon Factor*, a young adult contemporary science fiction thriller that blends a murder mystery with cutting edge technology, and has appeared in a variety of anthologies such as *Legends of New Pulp Fiction*. He and his wife Brenda live in the wilds of Central Pennsylvania with their three children, who provide a great deal of inspiration for his work. Email him at wgcarey@1791.com.

INTERIOR ILLUSTRATIONS –

Clayton Hinkle —a life-long, self taught (for the most part) artist whose main ambition in life is to basically draw cool, adventurous, fantastic, horror-ific Pulp and Comic art. Most, if not all, of his published work has been in the new Pulps of today, Air Ship 27 Productions being the major outlet of his wares by far, as well as work for the fanzine "REH, Two-Gun Raconteur", a 'zine dedicated to the late, great Robert E. Howard and his works. He hopes to one day make his living by drawing, pure and simple.

COVER ARTIST –

Graham Hill— Sometime Comic-book cover artist for small press publishing companies. Recently completed covers for BLUEWATER COMICS on their Freddie Mercury (Queen front man), David Bowie and other graphic novels. (Brain May from the band Queen apparently liked the Freddie one...not sure what the "Thin White Duke" thought of his ...) Covers for magazines such as SIMIAN SCROLLS, APE CHRONICLES, BLOKES TERRIBLE TOMB OF TERROR. Earned a first class BA (Hons) degree in fine art many years ago when I had more hair. Can be found on Face Book where I sometimes go under the Pseudonym of "Cover Monkey" https://www.facebook.com/CoverMonkeyGrahamHill

www.ingramcontent.com/pod-product-compliance
Lightning Source LLC
Chambersburg PA
CBHW051136260626
47170CB00005B/1841